THE TIME OF THE FLOOD

The Northumbrian village of Carlton is hit by unprecedented flooding when torrential rain overwhelms its defences and the river bursts its banks. During a long and difficult night, Anna Mason and her friend David Wilson work together to help the needy. Meanwhile, moody Gregory McKenzie, the attractive visiting grandson of one of the villagers, shows a previously unsuspected side to his character. But the flood will also wash away decades of secrecy, unearthing old family mysteries . . .

Books by *Miranda Barnes*
in the *Linford Romance Library:*

DAYS LIKE THESE
A NEW BEGINNING
IT WAS ALWAYS YOU
THE HOUSE ON THE HILL
MYSTERY AT CASA LARGO
ORKNEY MYSTERY

MIRANDA BARNES

THE TIME OF THE FLOOD

Complete and Unabridged

LINFORD
Leicester

First published in Great Britain in 2017

First Linford Edition
published 2018

A catalogue record for this book is available
from the British Library.

ISBN 978–1–4448–3746–9

Published by
F. A. Thorpe (Publishing)
Anstey, Leicestershire

Set by Words & Graphics Ltd.
Anstey, Leicestershire
Printed and bound in Great Britain by
T. J. International Ltd., Padstow, Cornwall

This book is printed on acid-free paper

1

'You don't have to worry about me, dear.'

'No, of course I don't,' Anna said with a smile. 'You're as tough as old boots, aren't you?'

Liza Tully, pushing ninety now, cackled with delight. 'You're right there. I am. It will take more than a bit of rain to worry me!'

'Well, that's good to know. So when there's two feet of water in your kitchen, you're not going to be bothered?'

The old lady shook her head. 'I'll just move upstairs. I can take a kettle with me, so I can have a hot drink. I'll be perfectly all right.'

Anna rolled her eyes. You couldn't help but admire the spirit, but she really hoped it wasn't going to be tested. The old folk were a lovely lot, but the weather forecast and the flood warnings were more serious than she could recall. The village was going to have a difficult few days if the forecasters were right, and these days they usually were about the big weather events. It was just that sometimes their timing was out, so that the next weather system arrived early or late.

'I must be going now, Liza. Is there anything I can get you? Anything you need from the shops?'

'My prescription. Could you collect that for me from the surgery? Oh, I need some bread buns as well. Not the hard ones with seeds on. I like the soft ones with . . . '

'I know, I know! I'll get you some. Anything else?'

'I don't think so, thank you.'

'Milk? How are you off for milk?'

'You'll have to look in the fridge, pet. I'm not sure.'

There wasn't any milk in the fridge. In fact, there wasn't much of anything in the fridge, or anywhere else either.

Anna grimaced. She had better make a list of the things she thought were needed. Liza had no idea what she had. Food and eating didn't seem to be very high on her agenda these days.

I'll do that, make a list, she thought. And I'll collect the things for Liza. Then I must get away home. First, though, she'd better just check around the cottage, and make sure the water wasn't getting in anywhere. This rain was going to test a lot of folks' houses.

Thankfully, everything seemed to be all right so far. Rainwater was sluicing through the yard and puddling in the little front garden, and she could hear it pouring off the roof and gurgling down the pipes, but the inside of the cottage was still dry and warm. That was a relief. Getting somebody to attend to a leaking roof might be next to impossible over the next few days.

'Ship-shape and dry, Liza,' she announced, returning to the kitchen. 'We don't even need to get the buckets out. Your cottage is better than mine

3

when it comes to wet weather.'

'Well, it's got a good roof,' Liza said. 'My Tom did it himself, and when he did something it was done properly.'

A long time ago, though, Anna thought. Liza's husband had been gone thirty years or more. Still, he must have done a good job.

'I'll be away now, Liza. I'll collect those things for you from the village, but I may not get back here tonight. Will you be all right, do you think?'

'Of course I will! You don't need to be fussing after me, not at your age. You get away to your young man!'

'My young man? That'll be the day.'

'What? You don't have one?'

'Not at the moment, Liza, no.' And not for a long time, actually, she thought with a wry smile.

'Well, you should have. A lovely girl like you?'

'Chance would be a fine thing, Liza.'

'What's chance got to do with it? You've got to go looking! Make it happen. Good men don't grow on trees, you know, and none of us is getting any younger. Anyway, off you go — and don't you worry about me!'

Anna was glad to escape.

2

She made her way into the village centre, ducking her head against the sheets of rain blowing down the hillside, and wishing she had a better coat for wet weather. This one she was wearing was too short, and it wasn't waterproof either. She was going to be absolutely soaked by the time she got home.

After visiting the GP surgery and the Co-op for Liza, she decided to call on Willie McKenzie to make sure he was all right. The carers who came to see to him might be unable to get here in this weather. Even if the roads were still open, the worry for them would be whether they would be able to get back home again afterwards. That might stop them coming.

Willie McKenzie lived in a stone cottage just off the village green. His wasn't a big house, but it was a home big with character and history. Like Willie himself, she thought with a smile. He was just like Liza, and very nearly the same age. It must have been something they put in the water when they were children, the way these old ones kept going. They kept their spirits up whatever the circumstances. They were a grand bunch.

Another fierce squall made her duck her head and pull the hood of her jacket closer. She grimaced as she felt cold drops of rainwater slide down her back. Never mind! She would have a hot bath when she got home. That would sort her out.

When would that be, though? It had been a long and difficult day already. For a moment, she considered going straight home, but only for a moment. She still had things to do, and people to see who needed her help.

Oh dear! she thought as she approached Willie's cottage and recognised the posh car standing outside. His grandson must be visiting. What a pity. Willie was a grand old chap, but Gregory was a different matter.

It wasn't that she seriously didn't like him, or that she had ever fallen out with him. She didn't know him well enough for that. It was more a matter of him not being very friendly and being difficult to talk to. She never knew quite what to say to him. He didn't seem to know what to say to her either, if it came to that. So it cut both ways, she supposed. All the same, she never felt welcome when Gregory was around. Thankfully, that didn't seem to happen very often.

She slowed to a stop and hesitated. Should she give Willie a miss today? After all, he did have company. Then the door opened and she lost the chance. Gregory appeared. He peered out into the rain and saw her, making it too late to withdraw. She had to at least say something.

'Good evening, Mr McKenzie. How are you today?'

'I've been better,' he said reluctantly.

'Oh, it's just the weather! We're all waiting for the sun to shine again.'

The way he looked at her then, she wished the ground would open up and swallow her. She felt like an utter idiot. If only she could have managed to arrive five minutes later! Gregory would have been gone by then, and she wouldn't have had to go through this ordeal. It was like running the gauntlet.

'The weather, is it?' he said with a scornful laugh, shaking his head.

That made her feel even worse. But she was determined to stand her ground. You couldn't buckle in front of a condescending, overbearing man. Oh, no. Not her!

But, to her surprise, he then wrong-footed her by asking her how she was. She was astonished. Gregory wasn't a man who had ever seemed much interested in other people, and had never seemed to regard her as anything but an irritating nuisance.

'Wet, but still functioning, thank

9

you,' she told him.

'You'll have come to see my grandad again, I suppose?'

'Yes, I have. If it's convenient?'

Gregory just shrugged. 'I don't know why you bother.'

'I just wanted to make sure he was all right in this terrible weather.'

'The weather's not going to affect him, is it? He's never been out of the house.'

'No, I don't suppose he has. He's not very mobile at the best of times.'

'The best of times?' Gregory said, shaking his head. 'When are they?'

Anna was suddenly irritated. She didn't know if Gregory was poking fun at her or his grandfather, but either way she was hearing his scorn for one or the other of them, and she didn't like it.

'Mr McKenzie, your grandfather is very elderly, as you know, and he's not a well man. He simply can't go gallivanting about any more!'

That prompted more mirth and headshaking. 'Gallivanting!'

10

'Anyway,' Anna said, calming down, 'how is he today?'

'The same. Complaining about everybody and everything in the world. I don't know why you bother coming to see him. He depresses me.'

'I'm his elder at church, Mr McKenzie. The church tries to looks after its members, as well as others in the community, and he's one of the half-dozen less able folk I keep an eye on. Besides, I like your grandfather. He's a good man.'

'He's not good for much now!'

'I shall assume you're just joking, Mr McKenzie,' she said crisply. 'Now, may I go inside to see your grandfather, please?'

'Help yourself,' Gregory said, chuckling. 'I'm just leaving. Mind he doesn't bite!'

'I hardly think that's likely. He's resisted the temptation so far. Not a hint of savage behaviour at any time.'

'No? He must keep it all for me.'

3

When she entered the living room, Willie was in the chair near the window, where he liked to sit and look out at the garden. On days like this it wasn't a very enticing prospect, but it was still better than staring at four blank walls.

'It's just me, Willie!' she called from the doorway. 'I'm not disturbing you, am I?'

'Hello, pet!' he replied with a smile. 'Come on in. I was just wondering if I would see you today.'

'You very nearly didn't. The water gushing down the hillside almost washed me away.'

'Some storm, isn't it? My grandson Gregory has just left. I hope he can get back to Newcastle all right.'

'Yes, I just saw him. Oh, he'll be all right. I haven't heard that any of the roads are closed — yet,' she added. 'But there's plenty more rain to come, I think.'

'You're right there. This is a big one, this storm. The village could be underwater by tomorrow morning.'

'Oh, don't say that! I've got to get to work.'

'I've seen it before,' Willie continued. 'They say something daft, like it's a once-in-a-hundred-years storm. It happens, and it's over and done with, and everyone thinks they're safe now for another hundred years. So what happens?'

'We get another one.'

'Exactly!' Willie said with satisfaction. 'Statistics, eh?'

'They must be some use,' Anna said dubiously.

'Well, when you've thought of one, let me know,' Willie said, chuckling. 'Anyway, if I were you, I'd forget about going to County Hall tomorrow. Even if you manage to get there, you might not get back.'

Anna worked for Northumberland

County Council, and was based in the HQ in Morpeth, a small town some twenty miles away.

'I'll have to go,' she said. 'I'll lose my job if they can't rely on me whenever there's a bit of rain.'

'And what is it you do when you get there? Remind me.'

'Oh, important stuff, like filing and answering the phone. Things like that.'

'And they can't wait?'

'Oh, no! I help keep things in order, Willie. Where would the world be without the little people like me to keep things tidy and organised?'

'I don't know, I'm sure,' he said, looking up and smiling. 'But don't you go belittling yourself. You brighten my day, Anna. You really do. I don't know what I would do if I didn't have your visits to look forward to.'

'Nonsense!' she said, colouring with embarrassment. 'You've got Gregory, haven't you? He comes to see you.'

'Once in a blue moon, when he can't think of anything else to do. Anyway, he lives too far away. I can't rely on him. Not only that, either. You put a smile on my face, Anna; Gregory takes it off again. He's a right miserable so-and-so these days.'

'Willie McKenzie!' she said sternly. 'You can't say things like that. Gregory is a fine young man. And he does visit you. That's more than some of the young folk do around here with their parents and grandparents.'

'But does he put a smile on your face?'

'Well . . . '

'I rest my case,' Willie said, laughing.

'You're a wicked man, Willie McKenzie! You really are,' she said, trying hard not to laugh with him. 'Anyway, I have to go now. I just popped in to see if you were all right. Is there anything you need? Anything from the shops?'

'No, thanks. I appreciate you asking, though, I do. And I appreciate you calling in. You just get away home now — and forget about going to work tomorrow! The County Council will survive.'

'Oh, I don't know about that. Are you sure?'

'It's been there since before I was born. That should tell you something.'

She laughed, and came away from Willie McKenzie's house with a smile on her face, the encounter with Gregory quite forgotten.

4

She found the rain hadn't slackened off at all when she got outside. If anything, it seemed to have increased in intensity. She ducked her head against both rain and wind, and set off as quickly as she could manage. There were still things she had to do before she could head home to change out of her wet clothes and sort out some tea for herself.

First, she called in at the Co-op and the surgery to collect a few of the things that Liza had requested. Then she made her way to the URC church to see what was happening there. At times like this, it became a sort of informal drop-in centre for volunteers to gather. They were the people who did their best to keep the community going by looking out for those less fortunate, and those not so able to look after themselves.

There were the usual familiar faces

there when she arrived, people who could be relied on to help out at times of need. At their core, also as usual, was David Wilson, who had recently taken over the role of church secretary. These days, given that there was no longer a resident minister to take charge, it was a demanding role. Anna sometimes wondered how David ever managed to find the time to do his real job — the one he was paid to do, the one that kept a roof over his head.

'Anna!' he called, spotting her. 'Just the person I hoped to see — and needed to see!'

'Hello, David,' she replied, smiling. 'Why? What have I done?'

'Do you really need a list?' he asked with a grin.

'No, I don't, thank you very much! So what's going on, David? I've just got back from work, and I thought I'd see if anyone was here before I went on home.'

'Plenty going on, I can tell you. Doris!' he called to an older woman who was placing cups on saucers at a nearby table. 'Doris, can you manage on your own? I need Mary to help collect Mrs Phillips.'

'Of course I can manage!' Doris said indignantly. 'Mary's not much use anyway,' she added under her breath.

'Doris!'

Anna smiled, and turned away to hide it. Doris and Mary were the usual tea-providing crew, and the one was every bit as useful as the other. It was just that Doris liked to think of herself as the supervisor, and Mary wasn't prepared to concede that role.

'No, don't go, Anna!' David said, turning back to her. 'I really do need you here.'

'I'm not going anywhere, David. It's just that — honestly, those two!'

Somehow, she managed not to say that for once she wasn't in the mood for the Doris-Mary comedy show. She was too tired, too wet, and too hungry.

'I know, I know,' David said with a wry smile. 'But their hearts are in the right place. And they always turn up, don't they? We do need them.'

It was all true, Anna knew that. They did need people to make the tea, butter the scones and provide the biscuits, and somehow Doris and Mary always got the job done, despite their bickering.

'How can I help?' she asked, cutting to the chase.

'Where to start?' David said, running his eyes down his to-do list before he answered. 'We've really got a lot on this time. Bill Tait, the chairman of the parish council, has asked me if I can coordinate things, because our hall is the biggest space available in the village. Also, we have lots of pairs of hands willing to help, and he knows that.'

'Goodness! That's a lot to ask, David.'

'It's all right. We can manage. Anyway, most of the members of the parish council are getting on a bit, and they don't have an army of volunteers waiting in the wings to help.'

'I'm not sure we have either. An army of volunteers?'

David smiled. 'Perhaps I exaggerate. But we do have people we can call on — you, for example.'

'Thank you, David — I don't think!'

'To make matters worse — or different, at least — Bill tells me that when he got on to the County Council, asking what support they were going to provide, they basically said none for the moment. They're fully stretched, and have no spare capacity. Could we manage on our own until tomorrow?'

'And Bill Tait told them what? Yes?'

'You've got it!' David looked troubled for a moment. Then he drew breath, grinned, and said, 'Daunting, or what?'

'Oh, David! What if people start having heart attacks or breaking their legs? What then?'

'We'll have to break into the library, and get out a book on first aid. Seriously? Well, we do have a couple of nurses living in the village. I'm sure they'll respond if needed. And if it comes to something really difficult, perhaps the air ambulance will come.'

'If it isn't fully engaged in Newcastle, Sunderland, Middlesbrough — and I don't know where else!'

'The Air-Sea Rescue Service, then. They have helicopters, don't they?'

Anna shook her head in frustration. It was all too much. Helping people was one thing, but operating as a quasi-government and health service combined was something altogether different.

'Anna?' David said tentatively.

She sighed. 'Tell you what, David. Let's just get on with it, and face up to problems when and if they occur. How would that be?'

'A splendid suggestion!' David said, a big smile of relief spreading across his face. 'I knew I could count on you.'

'Now, what wants doing? How can I help?'

5

'Do you know Miss Fenwick?' David asked, peering at his list. 'Miss Elizabeth Audrey Fenwick?'

'Well, I know where she lives. Not far from me, as it happens. But I've never actually met her, I've just heard one or two of the neighbours mention her. Why?'

'We can't get a reply from her on the phone. Could you visit her, and see if she's all right? See if she needs anything, or if she wants to come down here with us.'

'Yes, of course. She's quite elderly, isn't she?'

He nodded. 'I'm a little worried about her. She's quite isolated where she lives. And if any houses are going to be flooded and cut off, hers will be amongst them.'

'What about me and *my* house,

David?' she asked with a straight face, teasing him. 'Will you come to see if I'm all right?'

He laughed and gave her a hug. 'Gladly, Anna! You know that.'

'Let me go and see Miss Fenwick,' she said with a chuckle, pushing him away.

She was still smiling as she left the church. A blast of icy rain had her ducking her face as she turned to head for home, but it didn't quash her good spirits. David was lovely. He really was. He spent his life helping other people, and he was always so good-humoured. It was such fun to be with him, too. They got on so well together.

Now, though, she had a job to do, and she had better get on with it. From all accounts, visiting Miss Fenwick wasn't an easy or straightforward task. The old lady was famously reclusive, and inclined to be impatient with people. Basically, it seemed she desired to be left alone. That was entirely reasonable and understandable, but at a time like this it might not be sensible.

David was right to be concerned about her. Miss Fenwick's house was in a very vulnerable position if it came to flooding. Someone really ought to check on her. Guess who seemed to have drawn the short straw! she thought with a wry smile.

First, though, she wanted to go home and change. Everything she was wearing was thoroughly saturated by now. She was feeling cold, too. No good would come of spending more time in wet clothes.

She left the main street and set off up a narrow path leading to Hillside Road, where she lived in the little place she had inherited from her grandmother: Heather Cottage. Such a heavenly place in summer. Not quite so alluring just now, though. The hillside caught all the weather that swept across north Northumberland. At times, it was like living in the North Atlantic.

But she was so lucky to have the cottage, she thought, as she stripped off and briskly rubbed herself dry with a big towel before changing into fresh clothes. It was a long way from being perfect. She certainly knew that. And she didn't have the money to improve it, any more than Gran had had before her. It needed some work doing on the roof, for one thing, and then new window frames and a new central heating boiler. And that was just the start! Thinking about decor and furnishings would be a long way down the road.

It was a bit bleak at this time of year, as well. But it was home, and she really was lucky to have it. On her salary, she would have found it hard even to rent somewhere decent, and actually buying a house would have been entirely out of the question. Besides, in summer it was so beautiful up here. Even in winter, on a rain-free day it could be very lovely.

Sometimes, though, she thought what a pity it was that David Wilson wasn't more interested in her. If he had been, they could have got together and pooled their resources. Then they could have either done one of their houses up, or sold them both and bought somewhere that didn't need so much doing to it. Oh, well! she thought with a rueful smile. It wasn't going to happen. David wasn't interested.

She did like him, though, and he had always seemed to like her. But not enough, perhaps — not in that way, at least. Not romantically. And, goodness knew, there had been every opportunity! They had known each other all their lives nearly, having grown up here and gone to school together. Sadly, though, it seemed as if true love wasn't to be!

Grimacing at her reflection in the bathroom mirror, she rebuked herself for thinking such ridiculous thoughts. You're not a teenager, my girl! Pull yourself together. You're old enough to know better. At your age, you're supposed to be mature and sensible, and other desirable things as well.

David's not the one, and that's all there is to it.

Anyway, she concluded, she wasn't in the market for a man, still less a husband. She was quite happy with her life the way it was, thank you very much. *So there!* she added, sticking her tongue out at her reflection in the bathroom mirror.

The buzzing of her mobile put an end to her introspection.

'Any luck?' David asked when she answered.

'Luck?'

'With Miss Fenwick.'

'Oh, no! Not yet. I'm just about to head along to her house now. I came home to get changed into some dry clothes first. How are things shaping up down there?'

'It's pandemonium. I think that's the best way to describe it. More and more reports are coming in of problems, and of people in difficulty. The scale of it is becoming alarming. But we'll cope. We always do, don't we?

'I must crack on now, though. There's a queue of people wanting me to decide things, and do things. Try to see Miss Fenwick soon, Anna. I'm seriously worried about her.'

'All right, David. Don't worry! I'm on my way.'

6

Miss Fenwick's home, Hillside House, was a large detached stone building. It stood in a vast tangle of a garden that hadn't been manicured, or much looked after at all, for half a century or more. Hillside Burn ran close by, on its way down to the River Dove, which flowed through the centre of the village. Normally, the burn was a gentle stream that trickled its way sedately down to the river. But at times of heavy rainfall it could very quickly become capable of sweeping away trees, rocks, dead sheep, and anything — or anyone — else in its path.

On this particular evening, the burn was already a raging torrent overspilling its banks. Anna grimaced as she saw the white water cascading down the gully in the hillside and overflowing on each side. The noise was scarcely believable, and sheets of spray were being hurled high into the air. She knew that the river below, as well as the village itself, would struggle to cope with so much water being delivered at such speed and with such power. It was going to be a difficult night.

She hurried through the gateway of Sunnyside House and skirted the shallow lake that had already formed across the driveway and a large part of the garden. It didn't look good. She just hoped Miss Fenwick was coping, here all alone — if, indeed, she was here at all.

Even nowadays, big houses like this often had a housekeeper or some such person in residence. Sometimes, too, the person concerned had been in the family's employ most of his or her life. Not in this case, though. Anna knew from David that Miss Fenwick lived alone.

She pressed the button for the doorbell and stood pensively, listening and wondering. She heard nothing, and began to wonder if the bell actually worked. Better give it a minute or two, though, before trying something else. The elderly sometimes had difficulty getting to the front door — or anywhere else — quickly. She didn't suppose Miss Fenwick would be any different. She wouldn't be entirely arthritis-free, any more than anyone else her age was.

Turning round to gaze at the pool of water in the front garden, she didn't hear the door open. She heard the sharp voice, though. It made her jump.

'Yes? What is it?'

She spun round to come face to face with a very tall, slim woman, who was certainly elderly, but equally clearly not at all decrepit.

'Miss Fenwick?'

The woman nodded. 'Yes.'

'Mr Wilson at the URC church asked me to look in on you, to see if you were managing all right. I'm Anna Mason, by the way. I live just along the road from you. Heather Cottage, if you know it? It was my grandmother's — Mrs Tait, that is.'

Miss Fenwick peered hard at her through wire-rimmed spectacles. 'To see if I'm managing? Why wouldn't I be managing?'

'Well, the weather . . . '

'It's raining. I know that. So what? That man!' Miss Fenwick snapped, seemingly exasperated. 'He is such a busybody. What on earth is wrong with him?'

Stung into trying to defend David, Anna said, 'He's trying to help people, Miss Fenwick. Mr Wilson is the church secretary, and . . . '

'I'm perfectly aware of who he is. But not everybody is a member of his flock. Surely you must realise that?'

Anna felt herself bristling now on David's behalf. 'Miss Fenwick, we're checking on all the older and less able members of the community, just to see if anybody needs help with anything. I'm very sorry if you see that as intrusive, but most people welcome our initiative. We just wanted to make sure you were all right. That's all.'

She turned and gestured at the expanse of water outside the front of the house. 'The burn is famous for flooding in wet weather, and your house is right in the firing line, I'm afraid.'

Miss Fenwick hesitated, seemed to count to ten and then said, 'You'd better come in for a moment. You can't stand there like this. Nor can I.'

'No, thank you. I must let David know you're OK, and that he can cross you off his list. It will stop him worrying.'

'Come in,' Miss Fenwick instructed, refusing to take no for an answer. She opened the door wide and stood back.

Anna hesitated, not sure she wanted to be any more involved with such a difficult person. There were so many others in the village who she knew would welcome offers of assistance tonight.

'Please,' Miss Fenwick added with a sigh, and that did the trick.

Anna stepped forward into Sunnyside House for the very first time.

7

Occasionally, in passing, Anna had wondered what the interior of Sunnyside House would be like. Although she didn't know Miss Fenwick at all — had never knowingly even seen her — she had passed by the house many, many times over the years. For much of the time it had appeared empty. Not lived-in, anyhow. Then she had heard that a new occupant, a Miss Fenwick, had arrived on the scene.

Very little had changed in consequence, at least on the outside. The house and grounds remained as remote and forbidding as they had always seemed, and Anna had seen nothing of the new resident.

Some people must have had contact with Miss Fenwick, but Anna had heard that she was seldom seen in the village. The people and things she needed came to her, apparently. So she lived in the village, but was not really part of it. Even so, like it or not, she was still a member of the local community, and Anna believed David Wilson was right not to overlook her at this difficult time.

Miss Fenwick led the way now into a large farmhouse-style kitchen with a huge oak table, a massive dresser and various other pieces of furniture, as well as the usual appliances. An Aga cooker occupied an alcove where once a fire would have blazed, or a traditional cast-iron range might have stood. Anna's immediate impression was that it was a lovely, homely kitchen, but that it really needed a household with lots of children to do it justice. It was a traditional kitchen for a traditional country family.

Intriguingly, though, there were some very modern-looking pictures on the walls — paintings, not prints, she thought. It was possible that they were landscapes, of a sort. You could make out bumps that might be hills and strong lines that could be rivers, if you looked with an imaginative eye. Mostly, though, they seemed to be great washes of exhilarating bright colour. Yellows and blues, in the main, but some strong reds too. Together, the pictures brightened walls that might have been exceedingly dull without them.

'Please sit down, Anna. May I offer you a hot drink?'

'That's very kind of you, Miss Fenwick, but I really shouldn't stay. There's so much to do in the village.'

'Nonsense! Whatever is going on down there can wait five minutes longer. You need to warm up before you set off again. Coffee all right? Or would you prefer tea?'

Anna was surprised by the change of tone, which was very welcome. Reluctantly, she accepted that she would have to accept Miss Fenwick's hospitality. She would stay for a few minutes, at least. You couldn't rush old people. They just wouldn't accept it. They had their own ways of doing things, at their own pace, and the last thing she wanted was to upset an elderly lady who had recovered her manners and was trying her best to be hospitable.

'Coffee would be lovely. Thank you.'

Anna turned and gazed at the pictures with more attention. Such a blaze of colour!

'Who is the artist, Miss Fenwick?'

The old lady turned and saw where Anna was looking. She smiled.

'I was admiring your paintings,' Anna hastened to add. 'They are originals, aren't they?'

'Oh, yes. Definitely originals.'

'Who painted them?'

'A passionate young female painter, who is now a rather elderly artist who prefers to work in chalk and pencil.'

It took a moment or two for that to soak through. Then Anna put her hand to her mouth, and said, 'Oh! You? I had no idea you were an artist.'

'Good.'

'Well, I think your paintings are gorgeous. They really are. They seem to bring somewhere like the Mediterranean right into the kitchen.'

'Yes, well. That was the idea, I suppose. Something like that, anyway.'

That seemed to be as much as she wanted to say on the subject. So Anna sat down and watched with interest as Miss Fenwick moved about the kitchen organising their coffees. She was a little slow, perhaps, but she seemed adept and perfectly capable. She knew where everything was, and had no difficulty reaching the things she needed.

That was a relief, Anna thought. It meant it shouldn't be too difficult to get her into a car when it came to leaving, which it probably would do sooner or later.

'Do you manage for yourself, Miss Fenwick?'

The old lady glanced over her shoulder, teapot in one hand and kettle in the other. She smiled and said softly, 'Whatever do you mean, Anna?'

Anna blushed. 'I meant . . . '

'I know perfectly well what you

meant! You're wondering if I shouldn't be locked away in an old people's home at my age, aren't you? Waited on hand and foot for what remains of my life?'

'Not at all!' Anna blurted out with considerable embarrassment now. 'I just meant that . . . '

'*Is this old lady mentally and physically competent?* Is that what you meant?'

Anna shook her head desperately. 'It's just that this is a big house for one person to look after, and I wondered if you had help with . . . with things.'

Miss Fenwick laughed with what sounded like genuine amusement. 'I know how you young people think,' she said, gently now, shaking her head. 'Believe it or not, I was young myself once.'

She returned to the table with two coffees, sat down, and added, 'I have a cleaner who comes in two or three times a week, but otherwise I do look after things myself. And, yes, it is a big house for one person, but I do love it.

It's where I was born, you see, and where I lived as a child.'

'Oh, really?' Anna was surprised. 'You grew up here? I didn't know that. I had no idea!'

'Yes, I did. My parents built this house, when they were very young and newly married, and living here with them was a very happy time for me. I don't think I've ever been happier, to tell the truth. I had a wonderful childhood.'

Anna smiled, relieved that they seemed to have found safer ground.

'How long is it since you came back here? It's not that long, is it?'

'Several years now, I suppose,' Miss Fenwick said with a shrug. Then she smiled and added, 'I came home, you see. Eventually I came home. Lots of people do that late in life. They return to the place they once knew, and that they loved best.'

Anna sipped her coffee and waited a few moments before saying, 'Miss Fenwick, we really must be going soon.

Can I help you collect a few things you think you might need for a night away from home?'

'Whatever do you mean?'

Oh, dear! Anna thought with an inner grimace. Perhaps this was going to be difficult after all.

'Your medication, if you have any, for example. Warm clothes. That sort of thing. You really can't stay here tonight, Miss Fenwick. The water has nearly reached your front door already. Soon it will be over the threshold, I'm afraid. And there's nothing we can do about that.

'In a minute I'll phone David Wilson and have him send someone up here with a car to collect us. We'll go down to the church hall and join the other people there.'

'And do what? Spend the night in the church hall? Is that what you're thinking?'

Anna nodded. 'I think it would be wise. Safer, certainly. Unless there are friends you could stay with?'

Miss Fenwick shook her head. 'No, thank you,' she said firmly. 'I shall stay right here. This old house has withstood heavy rain many times before, and so have I.

'But you must make arrangements for yourself, of course. Do phone Mr Wilson, and have him send a car for you.'

Anna hesitated a moment. Then she decided to make the call. Hopefully, by the time a car came, she would have managed to change Miss Fenwick's mind.

8

Mike Thompson from the butcher's shop came up with his car to collect them. Miss Fenwick remained obdurate and refused to go. She was not leaving her house, come hell or high water, and that was that. Reluctantly, Anna decided they had no choice. They would have to leave her there.

As Mike said cheerfully, 'You can only help them who want to be helped.'

'Are you enjoying this, Mike?' Anna asked, irritated, as they got into the car.

'What?'

'All this bad weather and chaos, and having to abandon old people to their fate.'

'Well, it makes a change, doesn't it? Nothing else much goes on in this village.'

Anna humphed her disapproval and

sat in silence the rest of the way to the church hall. There was nothing more she could do about Miss Fenwick for the moment, but she was a long way from feeling happy about leaving her alone in that big house, with floodwater lapping at the front steps. Goodness knows what's going to happen in the hours to come, she thought with a grimace.

David frowned when she told him of their failure to persuade Miss Fenwick to allow herself to be rescued, but admitted it was no more than he had expected.

'She's a stubborn old thing, isn't she? I just hoped she would respond differently to you, Anna. Anyway, it can't be helped. And we have more than enough to do here.'

'Perhaps we can go back a bit later?'

David nodded absently as he consulted a sheaf of papers. 'Yes. Now, what next? Old Fred Baker. I don't think we've been to see him yet. Could you . . . ?'

'Of course. But isn't he on the phone?'

'Doesn't seem to be. Mind you, he's probably pretty deaf anyway. So it might not be much good phoning even if we had a number for him.'

'I'll go round. I think we ought to see about bringing Willie McKenzie and Liza Tully in too. I called on them both earlier. They were all right then, but the way the water level is still rising . . .'

'I'll send John round there with his Range Rover,' David said crisply. 'Don't worry about them. You go and see Fred. Take my car,' he added, fishing in his pocket for the keys.

'Will it even start, in this weather?'

'It should do. I've just had it serviced. If it doesn't, the Pearsons' boy has a kayak, I believe.'

'That's a good idea!' She grinned. 'Tell you what, David, I'll just use my initiative again. How would that be?'

'That's the spirit!'

On her way out of the hall, she

paused and glanced around. It was amazing how many people had made their own way here already. Either that, or they had been brought by volunteers running a virtual taxi service. She spotted a dozen of the older residents she knew. Some of them lived close to the river, where there weren't any hills for them to climb when they needed to go to the shops or the doctor's.

The downside of living on low-lying, flat land was experienced on days like this, though. Flooding was not an unusual event for people living along the riverside. The area might not always have been called 'the floodplain', as conservationists and the media referred to it these days, but that was what it was, and always had been. In the past, people had known that and respected it. Alongside the river was where they had their water meadows, not new housing estates.

As well as the elderly, there were a few mums with children in the hall. Most of the youngsters seemed to be enjoying the experience of being evacuated, no doubt because of it being so close to bedtime. For once, they were experiencing a story for themselves, not just hearing or reading about fictional children in difficulty.

'Hi, Anna! What are you up to?'

She turned to greet one of the women, an old friend. 'Hello, Fiona! You here as well?'

The other woman shuddered. 'When I saw the water coming over the steps at the back door, I decided it was time to get out. I'd have been all right on my own, but not with these two,' she added, waving towards a boy and a girl who seemed to be practising their martial arts moves on each other.

'Karate experts, eh? Doesn't that work on swollen rivers?'

Fiona grimaced. 'Not funny, Anna. Terry will go mad when he comes home and finds our new three-piece suite ruined.'

'He's away at the moment, is he?'

'For another week.' Fiona sighed and

added, 'Sometimes — quite often these days, actually — I just wish he would get a shore job.'

'He'll probably do that eventually, Fiona, but it's a bad time just now to be job hunting.'

'That's what he says himself. And he does have a good job, I suppose.'

Terry worked offshore, on a North Sea oil rig, doing ... Anna wasn't exactly sure what. It seemed to be a good job financially, but she could see that the three-weeks-on-and-one-week-off routine might not be great at times for a wife left at home with young children.

'I must press on, Fiona. David has asked me to go and see if Fred Baker is all right. He can't get him on the phone.'

'Oh? Maybe the line has come down.'

'I wouldn't be surprised.'

'David is absolutely wonderful, isn't he?' Fiona said admiringly. 'Just look at what he's doing tonight. All these people here! I know the parish council are supportive, and no doubt the County will arrive eventually, but right now David is the person organising it all.'

'He is. You're right.'

'I sometimes think what a wonderful husband David would make for some-one. If I didn't have Terry . . . Even then . . . ' Fiona finished wistfully.

'Stop it!' Anna said, laughing. 'Just stop it!'

'But you're not married yet, Anna, are you?' Fiona asked innocently, turning to her with a grin. 'Have you ever thought . . . ?'

'I'm going — right now!' Anna said. 'I'll see you later.'

When she got outside, she saw the rain hadn't stopped. Nor had the wind. In the yellow light from the sodium street lamps, she watched the horizontal rain sweeping across the market square in sheets. She paused for a moment and shuddered. What a night!

Most of the centre of the village seemed to be underwater now; and what a strange, frightening picture it made. Briefly, she thought of Miss Fenwick, and hoped she was all right, but the old lady had made her views quite clear and had made her choice. For now, at least, she would have to live with it.

She grimaced and zipped up her coat. She had better get on and see Fred Baker. In Mike's words, she thought reluctantly, she could only help them who wanted to be helped. She just hoped they were all going to cope on this terrible night. In her lifetime there had never been anything as bad as this threatened to be.

David was doing his very best, but would it be enough? She wasn't confident about the answer to that question, but what she did know was that she would give him all the support she could. He deserved nothing less.

9

Anna's question to David about whether his car would work had been a serious one. His old Volvo started when it felt like it, and it didn't seem to appreciate wet — or even damp — weather very much. So she assumed she would be walking to Fred Baker's house. Wading, more like, she thought with a grimace as she stepped onto the flooded road outside the church hall.

But the Volvo was worth a try still. If Fred did want to come down to the hall, he wouldn't be able to walk, and she certainly couldn't carry him.

David lived in the centre of the village, in an old stone-built house at the end of a short terrace. It was handy for the builder's yard where he worked, running the office, and making a very good job of it.

The owner of the business was not

brilliant at paperwork, or being helpful and polite to customers either, especially on the telephone. Micky Charlton's strengths lay more in the area of putting one stone on top of another, and making the man who mixed the mortar for him work harder. So David complemented him nicely. Together, they made a good team, and a success of the business.

David's house didn't have a garden. Just a yard with a few containers and a raised flower bed at the back. But it did have space at the front for him to park his car, which was handy, especially on a night like this. There were no street lights at the back of the terrace, and Anna wouldn't have fancied poking around in the dark and the wet, trying to get the Volvo started.

The car was unlocked. David always said that, in the unlikely event of somebody stealing it, he would rather have the insurance money than the car itself. Anna had never really known if he was joking or not. The car certainly wasn't up to much, but David didn't have a lot of money to spare, and would probably have found it hard to buy a vehicle significantly better than the Volvo.

However, as she switched the ignition on and began turning the starter motor over and over again, with absolutely nothing to suggest the engine would ever kick into life, she decided David hadn't been joking about the insurance money. He had probably meant it. And with good reason!

Frustrated beyond belief, she could have wept. She pounded the steering wheel with rage, and in doing so accidentally hit the horn. The sudden unexpectedness of the harsh blast from it brought her to her senses and made her sit up.

Right! she decided. I'll just have to walk.

As she opened the door to get out, a voice came to her from the darkness. 'Everything OK? Are you all right?'

She got to her feet, stood upright, and turned to look for the person who had spoken. It was a man, one who was well-wrapped in an all-weather coat and hat. She wasn't immediately sure who it was, but there was something about the voice she recognised. She peered harder.

'Gregory?'

'Oh, it's you! Anna, isn't it?'

She nodded. 'What are you doing here? I thought you'd gone back home to Newcastle.'

'I couldn't make it. The damned road is closed — flooded. I got a long way down the valley, but then I had to turn back.'

She was surprised. 'It's unusual for the road to be closed.'

'Well, it is now. The police are not letting anyone through. They say it's too dangerous. Wimps that they are!'

'If they say that, it must *be* dangerous.'

'Why? What's going to happen? Vehicles going to get washed away? I don't think so.'

'It can occur, Gregory.'

He snorted with derision. 'Anyway, what are you doing? What's the problem?'

'I was hoping to take David Wilson's car here to visit an elderly gentleman who lives alone. We want to know if he's all right.'

'Not my grandad?'

'No. Someone else has gone for him. They'll bring your grandad over to the church hall. That's where people who have been flooded out are gathering. Go and see him. He'll be pleased.'

'No. I've seen him once today already. That's enough. I'm off to the pub now, to see if I can get bed and breakfast for the night. It's a nuisance, as well as an expense, but there's nothing else I can do.'

She almost told him again to check on his grandfather, but managed to curb her tongue. What good would it have done?

Instead, she said, 'Unfortunately, David's car won't start. It doesn't like wet weather. So I'll have to walk.'

'Well, I'm not much of a mechanic myself. So I won't be able to help start the car. But if where you're going is on the way to the pub, I can give you a lift?'

'No, thank you very much. I can walk,' Anna said bristling. 'I wouldn't want to inconvenience you. There must be a lot you need to do.'

She couldn't help the note of sarcasm that had entered her voice. This miserable man! Willie McKennzie was dead right about him.

'Not a lot to do, perhaps, but I did want to watch the football on the telly tonight.'

That did it. She could contain herself no longer.

'Don't you dare talk to me about football, Gregory McKenzie. Just don't! OK? Some of us are scurrying around in the cold and the wet tonight trying to save people's lives — including your grandfather's!

'There are people out there who may not survive. We all have a seriously difficult night ahead of us. So don't you dare talk about football to me!'

'Hey!' Gregory said, taken aback. 'Don't take it out on me. It's not my fault. I didn't bring the bloody rain!'

'Oh, get out of my way, you stupid, selfish man! I haven't got time to waste talking to you.'

She slammed the car door shut, pushed past him, and set off to walk, leaving him astonished and indignant.

'There's no need to take that attitude,' he called after her.

'Oh, yes there is!' she responded without so much as a backward glance.

10

It was a ten-minute walk to Fred Baker's house on the far side of the village. By the time she got there, Anna was pretty wet, but at least she had calmed down. Gregory McKenzie was banished to the back of her mind. There were more important things to think about.

As soon as she reached the garden gate, she could see she needed to phone David and have someone come to help her rescue Fred. The small front garden was under two or three feet of water from the main river, which had overspilled its banks. Fred's house had been one of the river's first victims, and now the water was halfway up the front door and had reached the ground-floor window sills.

Anna grimaced as she wondered what it would be like inside the house.

Oh, the poor man! She just hoped he had managed to keep himself out of the water. Had he been able to get upstairs? Was that a glimmer of light she could see up there? A candle, perhaps? She was pretty sure it was. Not a normal light anyway. With so much water in the house, the electrics would have failed.

What to do? She hesitated to approach any closer to the house, the way the water was swirling around so powerfully. She would have to wait until she could get someone here to watch her back.

Just then a face appeared at an upstairs window. She waved frantically. The figure waved back, and opened a window.

'Are you all right, Mr Baker?'

'Not too bad, thank you. But I'm trapped. I don't think I can get downstairs.'

'Don't even think about it! Stay right where you are. I'm going to phone for help.'

She called David and explained the

situation, stressing how urgent it was. He promised to send help fast.

Thank God! she thought afterwards. David hadn't panicked. He had simply listened to her patiently and dealt with it, no doubt while people were tugging at his jacket and shouting in his ear — and while he was making and receiving phone calls to and from all and sundry! That man deserved a medal.

The dark, miserable night suddenly became a lot blacker. All the street lights went out. Just what we need! Anna groaned despairingly. A power cut.

Well, why not? she thought with grim determination, squaring her shoulders. It had to happen. Bring it on! We'll cope.

It was amazing how dark it had become. Every visible light, apart from Fred Baker's candle, had suddenly been extinguished. Anna couldn't even see her own feet. But she could feel them, and hear them, as the swirling water pulled and tugged at her, and then climbed over the tops of her walking boots.

Wellies, she thought with a grimace. Ugh! Why on earth didn't I put my wellies on? Thigh waders, chest waders even — those things the anglers wore — would have been better still.

'You just hang on there, Mr Baker,' she called. 'Help will be here soon. David Wilson is sending someone with a vehicle to help me get you of there.'

'Then what?' he said, sounding distinctly unimpressed. 'This is my home. I can't just leave it.'

She closed her eyes for a moment, frustrated. Why was it so difficult to persuade people they were in deadly danger?

It's his home, she reminded herself sternly. He's told you that. It's important to him. Everything he possesses is in there, all his memories as well as his earthly goods.

'The idea, Mr Baker, is for people who've been flooded out to stay in the church hall. It will only be temporary. Probably just overnight. There's food and heating there. Lots of your friends, too.'

Mr Baker seemed dubious about that. 'Friends? What friends?' he asked suspiciously. 'At my age, you don't have any friends left, hardly. Mostly they're in the churchyard, my old friends.'

'Give me strength!' Anna muttered to herself. What am I doing, trying to cheer him up? It's me that needs cheering up now!

'Willie McKenzie, Mr Baker? He's a friend, isn't he?'

'Oh, aye. I've known Willie all my life. Is he there?'

'Yes, he is,' she said, lying desperately, and hoping she wouldn't be found out.

'Liza Tully? What about her?'

'She's there, as well — or she will be soon.'

Unaccountably, Mr Baker began chuckling. For a moment she thought it was a fresh surge of river water she could hear gurgling, but it wasn't. It was Mr Baker, amused for some reason, chuckling to himself.

'Liza was always a good turn,' he called cheerfully. 'I used to tell her she should be on the music hall stage. That was before the telly came in, you know?'

'Yes, I do know about music halls, Mr Baker. Like Balmbra's?' she asked with sudden inspiration, quoting the establishment which was mentioned in the Geordie anthem 'Blaydon Races'.

'Balmbra's? Fancy you knowing about that!'

'Everybody in the whole wide world has heard of Balmbra's and 'Blaydon Races', Mr Baker.'

'Aye. True enough, probably. But the fellow that wrote it never made any money out of it, you know.'

'Didn't he?' she said despairingly. 'I didn't know that.'

'Died in poverty,' Fred added in a satisfied tone. 'So I understand, at least.'

Anna rolled her eyes.

'Aye, well. Liza Tully, eh?' Fred continued. 'We used to make our own entertainment, you know, in the old days. We had to! There was no alternative. And Liza was the best there was at entertaining — in the village, mind.'

'I didn't know that, Mr Baker,' Anna said as patiently as she could manage. 'Singer, was she?'

'A nightingale! What a voice she had. She was a good comedian, as well.'

Anna rolled her eyes. Oh, come on, David! For goodness' sake, someone get here soon — please! I can't keep this up much longer. I shall go mad.

But if I don't keep it up, what then? Will old Fred panic and try to jump? How will I stop him if he does?

Moments later, as if in answer to her heartfelt plea, a big 4×4 vehicle turned the nearby corner and forged through the lake that the road had become, heading towards her, its brilliant head-lights showing the way through the darkness. What a wonderfully welcome sight it made.

'Here you are!' a familiar voice boomed through the open window on the driver's side. 'I was worried about you.'

'David?' Her relief at hearing his voice was almost overwhelming. 'Oh, David! Thank you, thank you! I'm so glad you've come.'

'Evening, Fred!' David called cheerfully up to the bedroom window as he got out. 'How are you doing?'

'Not too bad, considering.'

'That's good. We'll soon have you out of there. Just hang on a bit longer.'

David sloshed his way over to Anna. 'What's the situation?' he asked in a low voice.

She grimaced. 'The downstairs is obviously flooded. I didn't even like to try going into the house on my own, the water looks so powerful.'

'Quite right, too.'

'I've been trying to keep him occupied, keeping his mind off it. So

Fred and I have been talking about the old days. Music halls and things.' She rolled her eyes in a gesture of frustration at the absurdity of it. 'But somehow we need to get him downstairs and out of the house. If we don't do it soon, we may not be able to do it at all — not tonight, at least.'

'Well done, you,' David said softly. 'Thank you for coping.'

She gave him a tired smile, so very grateful for the support, but by then David had turned away to study how to get into the house.

In the end, they left the front door alone, and made their entry via a small window in the scullery at the back of the house. David broke the glass and opened the frame. Then he helped Anna through the gap.

Once inside, she opened a bigger window. Then she brought Fred downstairs, one step at a time, got him up onto a kitchen chair and onto the window ledge. David simply lifted him out bodily and turned to splash back to the car with him, David joking and the old chap chortling with amusement all the while.

Anna smiled with relief. She closed the windows and joined the men a couple of minutes later. Fred was in good form now, she thought. He was laughing and joking about how they had defeated the river, just as he had done all his life. She shook her head, still smiling. No harm done, she thought thankfully. David to the rescue once again.

* * *

Back at the church hall, it was busier than ever. Half the village seemed to be there now.

'The catering is going well,' Anna commented, seeing bowls of soup and mugs of tea everywhere.

David nodded. 'That's Doris and Mary for you. Like I said, they always come up trumps when they're needed.'

'Have they stopped arguing?'

'For now,' he said with a grin. 'It may not last. Right, Fred! Let's find somewhere for you to sit.'

'Oh, don't you worry about me, son. I'll find somewhere by myself.'

With that, Fred took off. Anna smiled. He was headed for a little group of people he must class as friends after all.

'Let's give the catering staff a hand?' David suggested. 'They're being run off their feet.'

She nodded happily. 'Anything that will help warm me up!'

'Oh, I could do that,' David suggested, 'given a little encouragement.'

She laughed and pushed him away gently. 'You're a terrible man! Get away from me.'

If only he meant it, she thought with a wry smile as she made her way through the crowd.

11

'Anna!'

She wheeled round to see who was calling her. It was Willie McKenzie, looking as happy as she had ever seen him.

'Good to see you, Willie. How did you get here?'

'A couple of the lads from the butcher's brought me. The water was getting too deep in my kitchen. I had to come away. I don't know what will happen to the old house, mind.'

'It will be fine, Willie. Don't you worry about that,' she said firmly. 'That old house will have been flooded more times than you've had hot dinners. It will just have to dry out. That's all. A little time, and it will be as good as new.'

The old man's face had been over-taken by a grimace, but now sunshine spread across it again. 'You're right there,' he admitted. 'This won't be the first time it's been flooded. I keep forgetting.'

'I see Liza Tully's here, as well.'

'Oh, aye. She was talking my head off. I had to move away and sit next to these lads, for a bit of peace.'

These lads! Anna thought with a smile. Not one of them under eighty, probably.

'She always was like that,' one of the group volunteered. 'Talking a lot, I mean. She hasn't changed much.'

'Well, she seems to have found plenty of company,' Anna said, waving across the hall at Liza, who was in the middle of a mixed group of children, mothers, and motley grandparents.

Liza waved back and said something inaudible. Anna just grinned, waved again, and moved on, looking to see who else needed help, or even just a friendly word. They were a good lot, she decided. And they were in good heart. They made her proud of the village community.

Although the electricity was off at the church hall, as it was everywhere else in the village, that didn't mean the place was shrouded in darkness. Far from it. Battery lamps and lamps running on gas cylinders gave the place enough light for people to be cheerful, and to see what they were doing.

The power cut didn't mean there was no hot food or drinks, either. The cookers in the kitchen ran on bottled gas, big red cylinders of propane. Heating might have been a problem had the hall been empty, but given the press of people and everything going on in it, Anna thought the need would soon be more for air conditioning than heating.

So we are well set up, she thought with satisfaction. It would have been nice to have some candles burning, as well, she thought wistfully. There was nothing like candlelight. But she didn't even want to suggest it. Candles would have been quite rightly ruled out on the grounds of the fire risk.

Looking around, she tried to assess if everyone was here who ought to be. Anyone missing? It didn't look like it, she thought with satisfaction. The volunteers and the elders had done a good job getting everyone here. The parish councillors, too. Everybody. How well they had all done!

David most of all, of course, she thought with an affectionate smile. He was the one who had pulled everyone together, and who was keeping their spirits up with his cheerful optimism and unflagging attention to details. Right now, he was lending a hand with passing out bowls of soup.

There was food for a day or two, at least, she knew. Not wonderfully appetising food, perhaps. Not gourmet meals, or even what one might choose in normal circumstances, perhaps. But good enough for folk who had had to abandon their homes in desperate times and were hungry. Good enough, too, to keep body and soul together, as they used to say. Hot chunky soup, bread rolls and plenty of hot drinks. What was wrong with that?

People would be fine, for one night at least. By morning, the outside world would hopefully have sorted things out and be sending in help. The rain should have stopped by then, and the floodwaters ought to have peaked. Hopefully, too, the electricity would be back on. Then everyone would be able to start thinking about drying their homes out and assessing the damage. Tonight, though, it was best not to think too much about all of that. Tonight was a time for feeling satisfied, and grateful, that those who had needed help had been given it, and were being well looked after.

Then, suddenly, she thought of someone who should be here, but didn't seem to be. Worried, she began circulating again, looking to see if she had missed her.

12

'David, is Miss Fenwick here?'

'No, I don't think so. Here, check the list.'

David handed her his clipboard. She found the list he had kept of new arrivals, and scanned it. Miss Fenwick's name wasn't there.

She grimaced and turned to talk to him, but he was already busy with someone else. She waited as patiently as she could, worried by the thought of a poor old lady alone in that rambling house as the water level climbed ever higher.

David was talking to John Angus, an agricultural engineer who lived locally, about how they might get heat into the hall if it got colder overnight. A local grain-dryer had space heaters that ran on propane, apparently. There were also paraffin heaters that could be borrowed from different places. It was an important matter. Anna curbed her impatience, and half-listened until she could reclaim David's attention.

'Miss Fenwick isn't here, is she?' he said when he turned back to Anna. 'What was the situation like up there? How bad was it?'

'The garden was flooded. The water hadn't got into the house when I was there, but it probably has by now. It was up to the front steps already. I'm seriously worried about her, David. She's on her own up there, in the dark and the cold — never mind the wet.'

David grimaced. 'Difficult, isn't it, when people won't accept help?'

'I don't think she realised how bad it was going to be. Nor did I, actually.'

'I know, I know! Nobody did a few hours ago. Look, take someone with you, and go and check on her again. Use that Toyota I had when we rescued Fred Baker.'

'Whose is it?'

'Don't you worry about that. I've

borrowed it from Micky Morgan for the duration. Here's the keys. I assume the Volvo wouldn't start, by the way?'

She shook her head.

David sighed. 'I'm sick of that thing! When my boat comes in, I'm going to get a decent car.'

'That will be never, then, will it?' Anna said with a smile.

'Probably.' He gave her a rueful smile. 'Away with you!'

She turned to see who she could find to go with her to check on Miss Fenwick. The trouble was that the capable people she could see were all busy and fully engaged. Other men she might have called on to help were not there, unfortunately. They were presumably out doing other things. And the younger women she could see all had children with them.

Her eyes ran around the hall. Then she did a double-take as she saw one man she hadn't expected to see here, and certainly hadn't considered. He was coming towards her.

'I didn't expect to find you here, Gregory. Have you come to see your grandfather?'

'Oh, hello again,' he said uncertainly. 'Well, after the shellacking you gave me, I thought I probably ought to check on the old chap. So, yes. That's why I'm here.'

'Good. Found him yet?'

She was not going to withdraw or modify the harsh words delivered earlier. There was far too much to do. Besides, they had been justified. She hadn't come across such a selfish man for a long time.

'I have, yes.' Gregory chuckled. It was the first time she had seen anything like a smile on his face. 'He didn't really need my company, though. I think he's quite enjoying himself with his old pals. Usually he's in bed by this time!'

Anna laughed too, if reluctantly. 'He's not the only one. I think there are a few of the older people in that position. Most of the children seem happy enough, as well, probably for the same reason — being up past their bedtime.'

She hesitated a moment longer, and then said, 'Are you doing anything right now, Gregory?'

He shrugged. 'What are you thinking?'

'I need someone to come with me to check on an elderly lady on Hillside Road. Everybody I would normally ask is busy at the moment, and I might not be able to manage on my own. Would you come?'

Gregory seemed surprised to be asked, which she thought probably wasn't too startling in the circumstances.

'Why not?' he said after a brief hesitation. 'I don't have any qualifications relevant to a mission like this, though.'

'Neither do I, or most other people here,' she said crisply. 'Come on, then! I've got the use of a four-by-four to get us there.'

13

They needed the 4×4. An ordinary car would soon have been stopped by the deep floodwater, but the Toyota had much greater clearance and power. It pressed on through the deep water without difficulty.

'This is great!' Gregory chortled from the front passenger seat. 'A lot different to the MG Midget I once owned. Did I ever tell you about that?'

'No,' Anna said, without any interest at all.

She was concentrating on the way ahead, wanting to be sure she didn't hit anything big and solid beneath the surface of the water. Broken and uprooted trees were easy to avoid, but submerged concrete benches would be a different matter.

'A classic car,' Gregory continued unabashed, 'but only a nine-inch ground clearance. If we were in that now, the water would be pouring over the tops of the doors. Just think!'

'Just think,' Anna said dutifully. 'But I don't know if we are going to be able to make it, even in this car.'

'I can't see why not,' Gregory said confidently. 'We'll be all right. The water might get under the bottom of the doors, but so what? A bit of water in the body of the car won't stop it. Besides, we've got wet feet already, haven't we?'

'What an absurdly cheerful man you are, Gregory!' Anna said with surprise, and a grimace. 'Don't you realise how serious this is?'

'What? You think this big lumbering thing will stop because there's a bit of water swishing around the floor? No way! The engine's not going to stop working. There's nothing to worry about unless the tailpipe gets submerged.'

Stalling was indeed something she had been worrying about. Now, with such a ringing assurance, Anna felt a bit better about it. If Gregory wasn't worried, why should she be? He probably knew a lot more about cars and engines than she did. Though that wouldn't be difficult.

'I've been able to drive for quite a few years,' she said, 'but I've never actually owned a car, and I don't really know anything about them.'

She regretted saying that. There was no need for her to tell this man, who she didn't like, anything at all about herself. Still, grudgingly, she had to admit she was glad of his company on this trip. The business with Fred Baker had shown her how difficult it was for one person alone to rescue somebody in trouble, which was what Miss Fenwick was likely to be by now.

'Cars are a luxury these days,' Gregory said nonchalantly. 'I have one, but I don't use it all that much — what with trying to save the planet, and the price of petrol. The Metro gets me most places I want to go, except if I'm on holiday or coming up to see Grandad. I don't really know why I bother owning one, actually. It's an expense I don't need.'

'Well, they're pretty much a necessity out here in rural Northumberland,' Anna said. 'Either you own a car, or you have to find someone to give you lifts. That is, if you must travel to work. It's all right if you're retired. The bus service, such as it is, is probably adequate then.'

They had reached the entrance to Sunnyside House. Anna slowed, turned, and stopped. The house was now an island at the centre of a lake of uncertain depth.

'Oh, dear!' she breathed anxiously, wondering if she dare go any closer.

'Can't see any lights,' Gregory said, peering through the windscreen. 'No candles or torches, I mean. Maybe she's left?'

It was possible, Anna thought. Miss Fenwick might have changed her mind and got out, despite being so adamant earlier. She could have made her own way, or someone — a neighbour or friend, perhaps — might have come for her.

'I hope she has gone,' she said anxiously. 'But we need to check. She might still be inside. We have to make sure she's all right, if she is.'

It was one thing to be alone in a warm, well-lit house that was your childhood home, Anna was thinking, but quite another to be alone in the cold and the dark, with floodwater rising rapidly all around you.

'Come on, Gregory! Let's go and see.'

Gregory hesitated, obviously wondering if it was really necessary, but he followed her as soon as she got out of the car. Together, they made their way cautiously to the front door, wading through the knee-deep water covering the driveway. Anna tried not to speculate about what horrors they might find inside the house.

14

The floodwater had reached the top of the steps leading to the front door of the house, and it hadn't stopped there. It had risen a good foot up the door itself. Anna hesitated, reluctant to try opening the door in case it was all that was keeping the water out.

'If it's this high out here,' Gregory said quietly at her shoulder, 'it will definitely be inside the house now. So go on — open the door.'

She nodded, knowing he was probably right. She tried turning the doorknob. It turned easily. She gave the door a gentle push. That was no good. The door moved slightly, but she could feel the weight of the water on the other side pushing back. Gregory put his shoulder to it and they pushed together, ineffectively.

'I can't believe it,' Anna gasped, standing back.

'There's a lot of weight behind that door,' Gregory said. 'Hundreds of gallons of water weighs . . . well, a lot!'

'Hundreds of gallons? That much?'

'Easily. Thousands, perhaps. Look at the depth of the water.'

She was appalled, and frightened. 'We've got to get inside, Gregory. I don't like to think about what it's like, but we have to see if Miss Fenwick's still there.'

'Unless there's a door set at a higher level at the back somewhere, we'll have to break a window.'

She nodded. 'That's what we did at Fred Baker's house. Come on! Let's take a look.'

If anything, the floodwater was even higher up the back door of the house, and the patio door of the conservatory.

'A small window, then,' Anna said.

Gregory identified one that was suitable. It was set high enough in the wall to be out of the water, but not so high as to be too difficult to reach. He dragged a timber garden bench over to stand on. Anna kept her torch focused on the window while Gregory tapped out the glass with a stone, and then reached inside to open the frame wide.

'We're in!' he said with satisfaction. 'You know, I could quite fancy being a burglar.'

'Gregory!' Anna said, irritated. 'Please take things seriously. We're breaking into someone's home. This isn't a game.'

'Yes, ma'am. I mean no, ma'am. Kindly follow me, ma'am. This way, if you please!'

She shook her head and grimaced. It was no time for jokes. Then she climbed onto the bench and followed Gregory through the window and into the house.

They found themselves in the kitchen.

'Miss Fenwick!' Anna called into the darkness. 'Miss Fenwick! Are you here?

It's Anna. I've come back to see if you need any help.'

The light from their torches revealed an appalling sight. The ground floor of the house was a lake. Dirty brown water was well up the walls. Its surface gleamed in a most evil, threatening way as it washed against the doors, and bubbled into cupboards and in and out of the kitchen appliances.

'I'm glad I found these welly boots,' Anna said, breaking the silence, referring to some old boots she had found in a cupboard back at the church hall. 'They may not fit very well, but I'm still glad to have them. I just wish there had been some for you.'

'A rubber dinghy would have been better,' Gregory said.

She giggled nervously.

They moved forward into the hall. No-one appeared in the light from their torches, and there was no answering call. All she could hear was the sinister sound of water swilling along the corridor and lapping against the main staircase — that, and also ominously drip-dripping somewhere.

A different sound, knocking, brought Anna swivelling round. Her torch revealed a kitchen chair bobbing up and down on its side, banging intermittently against the wall. She shuddered. It was awful, terrible. So sinister! This beautiful old house in a state like this.

'I don't think she's here,' she said in a small voice, eager to get back outside.

'Probably not,' Gregory replied. 'But if she is here, she'll be upstairs. She won't be down here.'

'That's true.'

'We'd better take a look.'

Anna was more than a little reluctant. It seemed like an invasion of privacy. This was still someone's home. What right did they have to go poking around in it? Besides, the big old house was decidedly spooky in the dark, with floodwater washing around in it. But she knew Gregory was right.

'Come on, then!' she said, wading

towards the foot of the stairs. 'Let's do it.'

At least I'm not alone here, she thought. I don't think I could do this if I was.

'It's a big house,' Gregory said over her shoulder.

'Especially for just one person.'

'She lives here alone?'

'Apparently.'

'Amazing. Just think of all the refugees a house this size could accommodate.'

'Oh, shut up, Gregory!' she said with a chuckle. 'You could say that about Buckingham Palace.'

'And frequently do.'

'Gregory!'

They climbed the stairs and tried the doors to several rooms on the landing. They found them empty, literally. Probably empty and disused for ages, Anna thought. Years, probably. Decades, even.

'This one looks more lived-in,' Gregory said from across the corridor.

She joined him and played her torch around the room. 'It's a sort of sitting room,' she decided. 'What we want is her bedroom. That's where she'll probably be, if she's here at all. Keeping warm.'

'Taken to her bed, eh? Yes. That's what I would do. Let the waters rise, but you keep warm and dry — for a while.'

'If you can't say anything sensible, Gregory, say . . . '

'Nothing at all?'

'That's right,' she said firmly. 'Oh, what's that?' she added, spinning round. She stood upright, listening hard, wondering if she had imagined it.

'It was a voice,' Gregory said. 'Come on! The next room.'

The adjacent room was a bedroom. It smelled used, was Anna's first thought, as she followed Gregory inside. Her eyes took in the cluttered furniture and the clothes strewn all around.

'She's here,' Gregory said with satisfaction.

Anna gasped as she saw the figure on the bed. Gregory was right. This was where Miss Fenwick had retreated. How very sensible. Was she all right, though? Alive, even?

Then, a moment later, all uncertainty was dispelled.

'What do you want?' a thin little voice demanded from beneath a mountainous quilt. 'Who are you? Why are you in my house? How dare you come into my bedroom?'

Anna smiled with relief as she heard the list of questions recited in such a cantankerous tone of voice. Yep! she thought happily. We're not too late.

'Miss Fenwick,' she said gently, 'it's Anna Mason. I was here earlier this evening, if you remember? I've come again to see if you are all right still.'

'All right? Of course I'm all right — and of course I remember you, I'm not senile. Get that bloody light out of my eyes!'

'Sorry,' Gregory mumbled, taken

aback by their dubious welcome.

'And who's this?' Miss Fenwick demanded, eyes glittering fiercely as she pushed back the edge of the quilt and lifted her head from the pillow.

'This is Gregory McKenzie. He came with me to help. The thing is, Miss Fenwick, as I expect you know, the floodwater has got into your house. The level is still rising as well. There's no heating or lighting either, I'm afraid, because of the power cut. So it's really not a good idea for you to stay here alone.'

'It's not a problem. I shall just stay here in bed until the electricity comes back on. We've had plenty of power cuts before. We've always had them in this village.'

'You can't do that, Miss Fenwick,' Gregory said firmly. 'Stay here, I mean. This is a major power cut for the entire district. It means no heating, light, hot water or hot food. It could be days, weeks even, before the electricity is restored.'

'How can you possibly know that, young man?'

'I'm an electrical engineer,' Gregory said firmly. 'It's my profession. I know the scale of the problem.'

'Possibly,' the old lady said grudgingly. 'Possibly you do.'

'I can assure you . . . ' Gregory continued.

Anna nudged him with her elbow to shut him up. She didn't want him standing on his professional dignity. This wasn't the time for a contest of wills with a stubborn old lady, when what they really needed to do was persuade her to leave her home.

Miss Fenwick wriggled up the bed into a sitting position, keeping the quilt wrapped tightly around her, and fixed her eyes on Anna. 'What alternative is there? What do you suggest?'

'I think it would be wise for you to come down to the church hall with us, Miss Fenwick. I know you don't like the idea, but quite a few people who have been flooded out of their homes are gathered there now. We have heating, lighting and food in the hall. So everyone is quite safe and well.

'Tomorrow, in daylight, we can assess what the damage is. People can take stock then and decide what to do for the best. Contact their insurance companies, and so on.

'But in the meantime — now, I mean — we really should move soon, while we still can. In a little while, the water may be so deep that we can't get our car through it.'

Miss Fenwick thought about it, but not for long. 'That's a very sensible argument,' she decided. 'Far more sensible than one is inclined to get from engineers and suchlike,' she added, with a sniff of derision in Gregory's direction.

Anna felt Gregory stiffen, and dug him in the ribs again.

'So I don't really have much choice, do I?' Miss Fenwick asked.

Anna shook her head. 'Not really. I'm sorry. Gregory, could you keep an eye on things downstairs, please, while I help Miss Fenwick pack a few things to take with her?'

'Yes. As a lowly engineer, I can do that,' he said. To Anna's relief, he said it with a smile.

'Now then, young man,' Miss Fenwick said testily, picking up on the comment, 'don't you be making fun of your elders and betters!'

Anna was even more relieved to hear that, too, said with a chuckle.

'Give me the car keys,' Gregory said. 'I'll fetch the car as close to the front steps as I can. Save us splodging through the lake.'

'Lake? What lake?' Miss Fenwick asked. 'There isn't a lake here.'

'There is now,' Gregory said with an even bigger laugh. 'Miss Fenwick, I must inform you that your garden has been converted into a beautiful lake.'

'Humph!' the old lady said. 'It's no joking matter, young man.'

But Anna suspected she was quite taken with the idea. It would be the artist coming out in her, she supposed. In a minute she would be wanting her box of paints.

15

Between them, they helped Miss Fenwick down the stairs. Gregory carried her across the flooded ground floor, and they got her through the window. Then he bore her round to the front steps and the waiting Toyota.

'I can walk!' Miss Fenwick protested. 'There's no need for you to carry me.'

'You haven't got any wellies,' Gregory pointed out.

'Nor have you,' Miss Fenwick retorted.

'No, but I'm used to wading through water.'

'Because of your work?'

'That's right. My skin is waterproof now.'

'Perhaps engineers are of some use, after all,' Miss Fenwick said grudgingly, as if she didn't really believe it.

'How would it be if I just drop you

right now?' Gregory said.

'You'd get splashed!'

'That's true. I'd better keep hold of you.'

'You two!' Anna said, laughing.

She was surprised by the rapport Gregory and Miss Fenwick seemed to have struck up. She hadn't expected either of them to reveal a sense of humour. But here they were, putting on a Morecambe and Wise show. What a relief! She had feared a battle between them. This light-hearted verbal jostling instead was making a difficult time much more comfortable.

She was grateful, too, for Gregory's physical presence. She couldn't have carried Miss Fenwick herself. Without him, she would have to stay in Sunnyside House herself!

The floor of the car was awash with an inch or two of water that had slipped over the sills. So they sat Miss Fenwick sideways on the back seat, with her feet up. Anna gave Gregory the keys to drive, and then sat with their passenger.

'You're taking far too much trouble over me,' Miss Fenwick protested.

'Nonsense! We're both wet already, but we're not going to let you get wet as well.'

'Well, it's very good of you. More than I deserve.' Miss Fenwick pondered a moment and then added, 'Will I know anyone in the church hall, do you think?'

Anna frowned. 'I'm not sure. Possibly.'

'I wouldn't want to be there all alone, you know.'

'No fear of that,' Gregory called over his shoulder as he got the car moving. 'You'll have us. Besides, the place is absolutely heaving. I never knew there were so many people in this little village.'

'Well, I don't like crowds either,' Miss Fenwick confided with a shudder.

Anna patted her arm. 'Don't you worry! It will be all right. You'll see.'

'If it isn't,' Gregory called, 'we'll move you to the pub instead.'

101

Anna winced as she anticipated the indignant response. 'You'll be fine,' she hastened to reassure their passenger again.

'What is that young man's name again?' Miss Fenwick asked.

'Gregory. Gregory McKenzie.'

'I see.' Miss Fenwick considered for a moment, and then said, 'He has some very good ideas, doesn't he? For an engineer, I mean.'

* * *

They got Miss Fenwick inside the hall, and then thankfully handed over the responsibility for looking after her to others. She was whisked away to a quiet corner by a couple of nurses who lived in the village and had come in to help.

'It's amazing,' Gregory said. 'All this going on here, in this little place. People really look out for each other, don't they?' he added wonderingly.

Anna smiled. She sensed a change in his perception of local life. 'It's always been like this. Surely you remember, growing up here?'

He shook his head. 'No, I don't. We moved away when I was just six or seven. My grandparents stayed, of course, but my parents moved us into Newcastle.'

'You never came back?'

'Occasionally, but not often. I grew up in the town, where our life was. Once or twice a year we'd come to see my grandparents — my dad's parents — but that was all. It's only since Grandma died that I've been making an effort to come more often to see the old chap.'

'Well, I can tell you it's appreciated, Greg. He's happy enough, I suppose, but it's a lonely life for him now he's housebound and on his own. That's why he likes me calling on him every day. He says it cheers him up.'

'I'm sure it does.'

As he gazed at her, Anna realised he meant it. She struggled to avoid blushing, but managed a small smile.

'I'm glad you just called me Greg,' he said.

'Oh? I did, didn't I?' she said with a nervous giggle. 'I wonder where that came from.'

'It's all right. I prefer it. None of my friends call me Gregory.'

'So now I'm one of your friends, am I?'

He nodded. 'You seem to be now. You weren't a couple of hours ago, mind!'

She laughed. 'Truce?'

'Certainly.'

'Good. Well, I'd better get on, I suppose. Thank you for helping me with Miss Fenwick, Greg. I could never have managed on my own, as you saw. I really do appreciate it.'

He shrugged awkwardly. 'I was glad to help. Is there anything else I can do?'

'You?' she said with surprise. Then her hand flew to her mouth. 'Oh, I'm so sorry, Greg! It just never occurred to me that you were available to offer help.'

'You need more hands, I can see that.

Besides, the power failure means there'll be no football on the telly tonight — no anything on the telly, in fact.'

'Go on, spoil it!' she chuckled. 'Tell you what. Go and see how your grandfather's doing. And I'll let David know we've got another volunteer.'

16

Whoever would have anticipated that? Anna asked herself as she walked away. She had a different perspective on Gregory McKenzie now. Actually wanting to help? It certainly made a difference to how she saw him.

But she shouldn't forget that he had been coming out here to see his grandfather on a regular basis. So he could never have been totally uncaring. She must just have seen him at bad times. Still, his performance tonight had been an eye-opener. She couldn't have managed without him.

Then there was the teasing relationship he had struck up with the formidable Miss Fenwick. The old lady had, understandably, been a sad heap under the quilt when they reached her. No wonder. She must have been terrified, there on her own in the cold and the dark, her home awash with floodwater. Probably very pleased to see them — or anybody! — but it was Gregory who had brought her back to life, and provoked those flashes of spirit and wit that had illustrated her strength of character.

You had to smile about it. That was the first time the two of them had ever laid eyes on each other, and how well they had hit it off! From the start, they had been on the same wavelength. It was almost as if they knew each other and were old sparring partners. An engineer and an artist. Blood brothers! She shook her head and smiled. Amazing.

Gregory's grandfather caught her eye as she walked past. 'Anna!'

She stopped to have a word with him. 'All right, Willie?'

'Aye, not bad. Quite a crowd here now, isn't there?'

'There is. Including your grandson. Have you seen Gregory?'

Willie nodded and looked quietly

satisfied. 'Oh, aye. He stopped by to see me.'

'Good. He's been helping me.'

Willie nodded again.

'He's been very good,' she added. 'I couldn't have managed without him.'

'Oh?'

'It made me think I might have misjudged him. Perhaps I've been too hard on him. Perhaps we both have.'

'Aye, well. You've maybe got something there. He was a decent enough lad when he was younger. Friendly, you know? Helpful. I always had a lot of time for him.'

She waited, wondering what had happened to spoil their relationship, but not ready to ask. Willie would tell her, if he wanted her to know.

'All that changed,' Willie said with a frown, 'after his wife left him.'

'Oh?' She was surprised. 'I didn't know he'd been married. You never said.'

'For a year or two he was. Then — you know how it is with the young folk these days — she upped and left. Something didn't suit her. Gregory, I expect. He wasn't what she wanted.'

'It seems a pity she didn't discover that before they got married.'

'It does, doesn't it? Either that or she should have stuck it out. In our day, you knew you had to do that. There wasn't any alternative. You stuck it out, and you learned how to compromise. You know?'

Anna shook her head. 'I don't, no. It just seems better to me for people to be sure of each other before they get married.'

'Aye, well,' Willie admitted, 'that's probably right. On the other hand, I'm not sure it allows for human nature. Folk change, you know, as they get older. They have to learn how to handle that, and still stay together.'

'What a wise man you are, Willie McKenzie!' Anna said with a genuine smile of appreciation. 'If ever I plan to marry, I shall come and talk to you first.'

'You could do worse, pet. You could. Me and Edith were happy together for an awful lot of years. By the way, I saw you and Gregory bringing someone in a little while ago. Who was it? Anyone I know?'

'Probably not. It was Miss Fenwick, from up on Hillside Road. Her house has been badly flooded.'

'Miss Fenwick?' Willie looked startled, and he kept quiet for a moment. 'Not Libby Fenwick, surely?'

'I'm not sure about her first name. All I really know is she lives in Hillside House.'

Seeing how pensive he looked, Anna said, 'Why, Willie? Do you know her?'

'How long has she been there?' Willie asked, ignoring her question. 'I didn't know she'd come back.'

'Oh, I don't know. Several years, I think. So you do know her?'

Again, he didn't respond directly. 'You'd think we would have known, wouldn't you?'

'Who?'

'Us,' he said vaguely, waving an arm to embrace the whole room — the whole community, perhaps.

Puzzled now, Anna said, 'I don't believe she comes into the village much.'

'No.' He shook his head. 'She won't.'

'But she tells me she belongs here, that the house was built by her parents.'

'That's her, then,' Willie said with satisfaction — and perhaps some other, more troubled, feeling. 'Thank you for telling me, pet. I thank you kindly.'

More puzzled than ever, Anna moved on, looking for David and another job. It was a little while, though, before she could get Willie's distracted face out of her mind.

17

'When we get this over with,' David said, 'I'm going to treat you to a slap-up meal somewhere nice.'

'Will that be fish and chips, or cheeseburger and fries?' Anna asked innocently.

'You don't think I mean it, do you?'

'Well . . . '

'I do mean it. We'll go to that posh hotel near Longhorsley. Or that seafood place at Craster. Somewhere like that. What's your fancy?'

She realised then that he wasn't kidding. He meant it. She doubted he could afford it, but he meant it.

'That would be lovely, David,' she said with a smile. 'But you'll have forgotten by the time this is over.'

'No way! You deserve it. And we'll do it.' He smiled, and added, 'If you would like that?'

She smiled again, and assured him she would. Goodness, she thought. What am I to make of that?

They were spending a few minutes chatting and resting. It was late now. So far as they knew, everyone in difficulty had been reached, and those who wanted to come here had been brought. People were settled. The children, and even quite a few of the adults, were sleeping — or trying to sleep. Those with airbeds and sleeping bags were best off. Others all had something — a duvet or a quilt, or even just blankets. Not everyone could be comfortable on a hard floor, of course, but people were making the best of things.

'At least they're all warm and dry,' Anna said. 'Apart from me, that is. Gregory McKenzie, too. We both got pretty wet tonight.'

'And a few others,' David said, glancing down at his own trouser legs. 'Do you need to change? We might be able to find you something. Stuff for the jumble sale, perhaps.'

She shook her head. 'If there is dry clothing, save it for those who need it. I can manage.'

David gave her a smile of gratitude, then went off to patrol the hall and see if there were any new problems for him to address. Anna smiled after him and shook her head. He had so much energy, and so much thought for others. He really was a wonderful man.

All the same, she thought with a twinge of regret, there probably wouldn't be any slap-up meal. He would have forgotten when the time came, or there would be some other sort of crisis for him to tackle. A posh meal with her would have slipped down his to-do list. That was David. That was his life. Those in need came first.

'Here you are!'

She spun round. 'Hello, Greg. How are you doing?'

'Pretty good. I've just been chatting to Grandad. Interesting. He was on about the old lady we brought in.'

'Miss Fenwick?'

'Yes. Libby Fenwick, he called her. Short for Elizabeth, I suppose.'

'What did he say about her?'

'He said he knew her when they were both young. She grew up here, apparently.'

'Yes.' Anna nodded. 'She said her parents built that house.'

'And now she's come back.' Gregory shook his head and chuckled. 'What goes around comes around, as they say.'

He paused, and then added, 'I don't know why, but I'm not sure Grandad is all that happy to see her again.'

'Oh, I don't believe that! What a thing to say.'

Gregory shrugged. 'Perhaps I'm wrong, but he didn't seem terribly enthused. Anyway, what happens next here?'

'We wait for morning, I think. Then we hope to see the Fire and Rescue Service, with their pumps and all their other specialised equipment. Perhaps the police and social services, too. Medics, as well. And people — builders, I suppose — will have to get out and assess the damage. Then there's the electricity to be sorted out . . . '

Gregory nodded. 'The lines will probably be down over the moors somewhere. It shouldn't take them too long to fix that, once they have daylight. A couple of days, if that's the only problem. All in all, though, there's a lot to be done, isn't there?'

Anne agreed with that. 'All hands on deck for the next few weeks, I think. It will be a while before the village is back on its feet again. What about you, Greg? What are your plans?'

He chuckled. 'My plans? My plans are all in the bin. I didn't count on getting caught up in all this.' With a shrug, he added, 'But here I am. I'll do what I can to help while I'm here.'

'Good. Thank you, Greg. Any further help you can give will be gratefully received, I can assure you.'

'I'll have to help the old chap get sorted out, at the very least,' he said with a frown.

'Willie — your grandad, you mean?'

'Yes. I wonder what his house will be like.'

Anna winced. 'Upstairs will be OK, of course, but downstairs will be a mess, I'm afraid. Previous experience tells me downstairs will be wet and muddy. That can be cleaned up, but drying the house out properly could take a long time. Months, even.

'Then the electrics will need sorting out, and furniture and kitchen appliances replaced. It's not going to be easy.'

'Who's going to do it? He can't.'

She shrugged. 'It will be the same as for everybody else, I suppose. A combination of family, community, local government, and . . . Don't worry, Greg. It will get done.'

'Paid for by insurance?'

She shrugged. 'I suppose so, provided people have house insurance. You'd better check with your grandfather and see what he has.'

'If anything,' Greg said with a sigh.

'Not tonight, though,' she said gently.

'Not tonight, Greg. The houses can wait till tomorrow. It's people we're concerned about tonight, remember?'

He smiled and nodded. 'You're right. That's exactly the best way to look at it. I think I'll see if there's any coffee left in that big urn over there. Fancy some?'

'Yes, please. I could do with a hot drink.'

They collected mugs of reasonably hot, and not too disgustingly stewed, coffee, and took them aside to continue their conversation.

'I meant to ask you,' Anna said. 'Are you really an electrical engineer?'

'As I told Miss Fenwick?' Gregory said with a grin.

'Or was that just to help get her out of the house, and into the car?'

'Would I lie about a thing like that?'

'Probably.'

He gave a rueful smile. 'You know me so well! But, yes, that is my trade, as it happens.'

'You're wasted, then. We should have you doing more important things than helping ferry old people to safety.'

'Not at all,' he said, shaking his head. 'I haven't felt so useful for a long time.'

'Where do you work?'

'Nowhere in particular. I work a lot from home these days. I'm a self-employed consultant engineer. Originally, I worked for Rolls Royce at Hebburn, but when they closed the works there I took the redundancy money and started up as a freelance.'

'I'm impressed.'

'No need to be, I can assure you.'

'Is it a successful business?'

'Financially, it is.'

'And you like the work?'

'I do. I got interested in electricity as a boy, when we had to do a school project on Lord Armstrong at Cragside. You'll know about him?'

'I should say so! There isn't anybody in this village who doesn't. Cragside, the first house in the world to be lit by hydro-electric power,' she recited. 'A lot more besides.'

'An awful lot. He really was a

pioneer. As well as being a major Victorian industrialist, employing tens of thousands of people along the Tyne, he was also an experimental scientist. There he was, late in life, still trying to fathom the magic of this new energy the world had always known about but until recently had never been able to capture or generate.'

Anna was puzzled. 'How did they know about it before they could generate it? I don't understand.'

'It was all around, everywhere — every time there was a thunderstorm.'

'Oh, lightning!'

'Exactly. People also experienced it when sometimes they rubbed something the wrong way, and a spasm of pain ran up their arm. Static electricity.'

'I've never thought about that before, but yes, I can see it now.' Anna smiled and added, 'You sound like an enthusiast, Greg.'

He laughed. 'Well, you're not far wrong. That was what engaged me as a young boy. Following in Lord Armstrong's footsteps.'

'And now?'

'Now I do big stuff. I help design power stations.'

'How interesting.'

He shrugged. 'Only to some of us. Not to everyone.'

Afterwards, Anna wondered what he had meant by that. It seemed an odd thing to say, until she remembered what Willie had said about Gregory's wife. Perhaps she had tired of his professional enthusiasm. It could happen.

18

A few of the older ladies were lodged in one of the smaller rooms off the main hall, to give them a little more privacy and quiet. There, Anna found Miss Fenwick, warmly wrapped in the vast quilt they had brought with her from Sunnyside House. Unlike the other ladies, she was not sleeping. Nor was she lying on an air mattress. She was sat up, but comfortably, on a very old chaise longue that Anna had last seen in a pantomime produced by the local amateur dramatic group.

'Hello,' Anna whispered. 'How are you?'

'Perfectly well, thank you.'

'Can't you sleep? Are you not tired?'

'Oh, I don't sleep a lot these days. Fits and starts, mostly. Besides, how could I sleep after such an exciting day?'

Anna chuckled. 'I know what you mean. I'm not in the mood for sleeping either.' She glanced around the room and added, 'If we were tired, we would sleep like everyone else, I suppose.'

'Possibly.'

'What do you do at home when you can't sleep? Read?'

'I paint, of course. Or I draw.'

'Really? At night? That's unusual.'

'Not for a working artist, dear. That's what we all do when we get the time — and there never is enough time.'

'Is that what you are? I didn't know you were an artist. Oh, dear! Not a proper one, a real one, I mean.'

'Why should you? But that is how I have earned my living all these years. Now, please go away, and leave me to think. There must be lots of people needing your attention more than I do.'

Anna smiled. The admonition had been delivered in such a friendly way that it was impossible to feel insulted.

'I'll see you later, Miss Fenwick,' she promised.

'Libby, if you don't mind. That's what I was always called here, in the village.'

'Libby, then,' Anna said with a smile, thinking Willie McKenzie really must know her. At least, he had done once, a long time ago.

'By the way, where is that young man who came with you to my house? I did like him.'

'Gregory? Oh, he's around still. Probably helping someone else. His grandfather, perhaps.'

'And who is that?'

'Willie McKenzie, a lovely man.'

Miss Fenwick chuckled. 'Willie McKenzie? Is he here too?

'Indeed he is. His house was one of the first to be flooded. Do you know him?'

'Not now, no. But I remember him as a boy.'

'I suppose you do.' Anna gazed at her thoughtfully, and added, 'He seems to remember you, too, Libby.'

'Mm,' Miss Fenwick said, neither

accepting nor rejecting the idea.

Anna thought of suggesting that in the morning Libby might like to meet Willie, but thought better of it. Had she wanted to do that, the old lady would surely have said so herself. Besides, there was a very good prospect of everybody meeting everybody else when daylight came, whether they wanted to or not.

She caught David at a bad moment for him. She was heading for a broom cupboard at the end of a long corridor, hoping to find a hot water bottle for one of the older ladies who was feeling cold. It seemed unlikely that she would find such a thing in the church hall, but it wasn't entirely beyond the realms of possibility. The cupboard was where the stuff that didn't get sold — at periodic jumble sales, Christmas bazaars, Easter fetes, and whatnot — tended to be put until it was brought out again for the next event.

Halfway along the corridor, she forgot all about her search for a hot water bottle. She saw a figure leaning against the wall. When she raised the torch she was carrying, she saw it was David. He was slumped against the wall, and trying to stop himself sliding down it.

'David!' she cried, breaking into a run. 'What's happened?'

She reached him, and grabbed him to prevent him falling. Then she eased him down to a sitting position on the floor.

'What's wrong, David?'

He gazed back at her and blinked, as if the light hurt his eyes, but said nothing.

She took hold of his head with both hands and looked into his eyes. He looked strangely vacant, his eyes unable to focus. She was very worried now. This wasn't like him at all. She feared something serious was wrong.

'Are you in pain, David?' she asked urgently.

His eyes steadied. He focused on her

and gave a gentle smile.

'Are you hurting?' she pressed. 'Are you in pain?'

'No,' he said, making a visible effort. 'Sorry, Anna. No, I'm all right. Just tired, very tired.'

Relief flooded through her. He knew who she was. He wasn't in pain. It wasn't anything like a heart attack.

'Tired?' she repeated gently. 'I'm not surprised. You've been doing too much. You're always doing too much!'

Somehow he found the energy to pull himself together and make an effort to get back to his feet.

'Just stay where you are for a moment,' Anna said, holding on to him. 'What we'll do is find a quiet corner, where you can lie down and get some rest. If you sleep, even for a short time, you'll feel so much better.'

'There's nothing wrong with me, Nurse,' David said with the familiar smile, but not in the convincing voice she knew so well.

'No, of course there isn't. But there

very well might be if you don't get some rest.'

It would have been no good leading David back into the main hall. There would have been no rest there for him there. She knew people wouldn't leave him alone for five minutes. There would always be someone in need of his immediate attention, or some urgent problem to address. Instead, she steered him into the kitchen, which was unlikely to be used much in the next few hours. David collapsed gratefully into an old armchair and went to sleep straight away.

Anna studied him for a couple of minutes and shook her head. She had never seen him as tired as this, but it wasn't too surprising that he was. She just hoped that was all it was. This was no time for an underlying serious problem to surface. Looking at him now, though, she felt reassured. Already he looked better.

Just in case, she would find one of the nurses to take a look at him.

Meanwhile, she would find a duvet for him. He needed to keep warm, just as much as everyone else did.

★   ★   ★

With David settled, Anna began to patrol in his place, feeling like the first mate on a ship who had been handed the bridge while the skipper took a well-earned rest. Strangely enough, she herself wasn't a bit tired. Not really. Sleep was the last thing she needed. Adrenaline was probably what was keeping her awake. When it faded, she would no doubt collapse in a heap, as David had done.

Oh, she did hope he was going to be all right! She couldn't bear the thought that there might be something wrong with him. Not David! He held the whole community up, and herself with it. He was such a dear man, she thought fondly. He would be all right. He would. He had to be!

She would pray for him, she decided.

The good Lord surely wouldn't let anyone so precious as David depart before his time. Increasingly often these days, she wondered if the faith she had held on to all her life was quite as strong as it used to be. The world seemed to be going to pot faster than ever. Not this little bit of it, of course. Not this village, and this valley. But much of the rest of it. When it came to a situation like this, though, she knew instinctively what the best thing was to do. She would look after David, and she would pray for him.

19

Willie McKenzie was asleep, and snoring, when she passed by. The sudden noise he made was like a volcanic eruption. She jumped and spun round.

Fred Baker, sitting nearby, caught her eye and chuckled. 'He's a noisy old bugger, isn't he?'

'He certainly is! He gave me a shock. I'm pleased he's been able to get to sleep, though. How about you, Fred? Can't you sleep?'

Fred shook his head. 'Not me, not with all this lot going on. Every time I start nodding off, I see the river rising and getting closer to my bedroom window. I don't know how to stop it, either — and I can't get out!'

'You won't be the only one having nightmares after this, Fred,' she said. She settled down next to him, sensing he needed to someone to talk to for a minute. Everyone else in the immediate vicinity seemed finally to have succumbed to sleep.

'We'll soon get over it, though, Fred. Once people roll their sleeves up and get on with cleaning up and repairing the damage, it will be a chance to get rid of a lot of rubbish and do some decorating.'

'I don't know how I'll manage,' Fred said. 'I can't do such a lot myself anymore. I could once, you know,' he said spiritedly.

'I'm sure you could, Fred. But as we get older, we all slow down and need help, don't we?'

'True enough. Mind, Willie's all right. He's got his grandson to help him.'

'His son, as well,' Anna pointed out. 'I don't know him, and he'll be getting on a bit himself now, but I'm sure he'll lend a hand.'

'I don't know about that,' Fred said, pursing his lips. 'They don't get on, you know? Peter never visits. Nor his wife either.'

'But at a time like this . . . '

'Aye, you're right. Decent folk let bygones be bygones, don't they? At least Willie's got them. I've got nobody.'

'Nobody at all, Fred?'

He shook his head. 'Our families, mine and Betty's, never did have many children. And me and her had none. That was just the way it was. We were happy enough, mind.'

He lapsed into a brooding silence that Anna decided she ought to try to dispel before the gloom set in.

'Do you know Miss Fenwick? She's another one, I think.'

'Another what?'

'Someone without children. At least, I don't think she has.'

'Libby Fenwick?' Fred chuckled, without sounding amused. 'No, that's not right. You've got that wrong, pet. She had a baby once. It was having the baby that got her into trouble in the first place.'

'Whatever do you mean, Fred?' Anna said, almost shocked by what threatened to be an unseemly exchange, but intrigued all the same.

'Of course I knew her,' Fred said bluntly. 'What's she got to do with it, anyway?'

Anna stared at him a moment longer, and then shook her head. 'It's just that I was thinking of Miss Fenwick because Gregory McKenzie helped me bring her down from Sunnyside House tonight. She's been flooded out as well.'

'Libby Fenwick, eh?' He shook his head and sighed. 'I'd heard she was back in the village. Are you saying she's here, right now?'

Anna nodded. 'In one of the other rooms.'

'Well, fancy that. I haven't seen her for many a year. I'll have to have a word with her in the morning.'

'I'm sure she'll be happy to see an old friend.'

'Old friend? I don't know about that, but I'll look her up anyway. How is she?'

'She seems fine. A bit shaken up, like a lot of other people, with her house being flooded. But otherwise she's all right. Wondering, no doubt, how she'll ever get the house sorted out.'

'She can join the queue!'

Recalling something Fred had said a few moments earlier, Anna asked, 'What did you mean about Miss Fenwick, Fred? She has children, does she?'

'I'm saying nowt more,' he said firmly. 'It's no good asking me.'

'Well, you did suggest it, didn't you?'

'And I shouldn't have. And that's a fact.'

Anna sighed and shook her head. What was wrong with a simple question like that, the kind that most people were very happy to answer?

'I'm puzzled,' she said.

'Well, ask somebody else. Ask Willie — when he wakes up. I'm going to get my head down now, and see if I can get some sleep.'

'Yes, why don't you, Fred? That's what everyone else is doing.'

She left him to it and wandered away,

bemused still by his strange response to her perfectly ordinary question.

A few minutes later, Anna joined Greg for another cup of late-night coffee from the big urn that never seemed to be exhausted.

'Ugh!' she said, turning her nose up when she tasted it. 'But at least it's hot.'

'Full of stuff to help keep us awake, as well.'

'Well, that might be a good thing. Most of the volunteers seem to be asleep now, like most of the evacuees. Someone has to stay awake. How are you doing, Greg?'

He smiled. 'OK. Quite enjoying it, actually. Perhaps I shouldn't say that, but I am.'

'Change of routine?'

'Something like that. Feeling useful, as well. I'm starting to understand why people like you get so involved in things like this.'

She shrugged. 'We live here. That's all. These people are our neighbours, and our friends. We know them all.'

'They won't all be in your church, though?'

'Oh, no! If the church had as many people as this in the congregation, David would be delighted. We all would!'

'He seems a decent guy, David?'

'He is. Very much so. He spends his life helping others. I don't know how he finds the energy, especially when he has a full-time job as well.'

'Rather him than me. I couldn't do it. I wouldn't want to do it.'

'No. It takes a pretty special sort of person, I think.'

She sipped her coffee and cast her eye around the big room. One or two people were stirring, but not many. The hall was full of people, old and young, most sleeping safely now.

'Old Fred Baker — the man David and I rescued — was saying that your father and grandfather don't get on. Is it anything serious?'

'Who knows?' Greg shrugged. 'It's been going on since before I was born.

I've never known anything different. Maybe they're just chalk and cheese, personality-wise.'

'It can happen, father and son.'

'True, I'm sure.' He yawned and added, 'There's been times when me and Mum wanted to bang their heads together. Still, I don't think anything's going to change now.'

'But you get on with your grandfather all right?'

'I get on with both of them. Sometimes I wonder how, and why. I've not been very good company at times in recent years. I've often come out here to see Grandad when I've been in a foul mood, hoping the change of scene would help — which hasn't been good for him or me. Perhaps I was in one such mood when you and I met earlier this evening?'

'I never noticed.'

'Liar!' he said, chuckling. 'You bit my head off for it.'

'That was only because I wasn't in a good mood myself. I was so worried about what was going on in the village. I didn't know how we'd cope.'

'Well, you did.'

'With the help of a lot of good people, yourself included.'

She was surprised to hear herself saying that, but she meant it. Greg really had been magnificently helpful as the night had worn on.

'When this is all over,' he said now, 'would you like to come into Newcastle for a day out, or a night out? See the sights. What do you think?'

'That would be nice. Are there lots of sights?' she asked, grinning.

'Mm. Plenty of them.'

'Whereabouts do you live, Greg?'

'I have an apartment on the Quay-side.'

'Oh? That sounds very swish.'

'Convenient is how I think of it. It's new, which means there's nothing needs doing to it. And being on the sixth floor, there's no garden to worry about either. Minimum maintenance, in other words. That suits me fine.'

'Nice views, as well?'

Greg nodded. 'Great view of the river and all the bridges. And it's handy. Right in the middle of the city.'

'Isn't parking a problem?'

'No. There's an underground garage, which is where my car stays most of the time. As I said earlier, I use the Metro for getting around the city. I only use the car for out-of-town work.'

'And out-of-town-fun?'

'Oh, well.' He smiled. 'There's not a lot of that. I work pretty hard. But, yes, I do go out sometimes. Anyway, come and have a look. Make your own mind up.'

'I shall look forward to that, and I shall hold you to that offer,' Anna said with a smile. 'I could do with a day out.'

20

Liza Tully was asleep, Anna noted with affectionate approval; but as she passed by, the old lady awoke.

'Anna!'

'Oh dear! Have I woken you, Liza? I'm so sorry. You were sleeping nicely.'

'Not sleeping. Just dozing, as usual. I seem to spend half my life dozing these days.'

Anna smiled. 'You're not the only one. Willie McKenzie is well away, though. He must be exhausted, poor old chap.'

'If he's asleep, I am surprised. He'll have a lot on his mind, will Willie.'

'Everyone here will. You all have flooded houses to go home to and sort out, but there's nothing to be done tonight, is there? Just get some rest. The main thing is that everyone's safe.'

Liza shook her head. 'I wasn't

thinking about Willie's house.'

'Oh?'

'That was Libby Fenwick you brought in here earlier, wasn't it?'

'Yes, it was,' Anna said, surprised.

'Well, then!' Liza said triumphantly.

'Do you know her as well, Liza?'

Liza nodded.

Puzzled, Anna said, 'Why would Willie be worried about Miss Fenwick being here?'

'I don't know, I'm sure,' Liza said smugly. 'You'll have to ask him. It's nothing to do with me.'

'Whatever do you mean?'

'Ask him.'

'Liza, I won't visit you any more if you don't tell me what you're talking about!'

Liza thought that over long and hard before saying, 'They used to walk out together.'

'Who? Libby and Willie?'

Liza nodded.

'That must have been a long time ago!' Anna said, amused.

'It was.'

'And?'

'That's all I'm saying,' Liza said firmly. 'My lips are sealed. It's none of my business, and I'm not one for spreading gossip.'

Anna chuckled. 'Not much, you're not! Liza Tully, you really are wicked, aren't you? But I do love you! Anyway, I must be off now. I want to see how David is.'

'David Wilson?'

'Yes. He was very tired when I found him an hour or two ago, and I insisted on him trying to get some sleep. I'll go and see if he's feeling any better. Anything I can get you, Liza? A glass of water? Another rug?'

Liza shook her head. She seemed to be thinking about something. Then, suddenly, she said, 'She had a baby, you know. It was all hushed up, but she did. We all knew.'

'Who did?'

'Libby Fenwick. Her with her high-and-mighty ways. There, now! And that's all I'm saying.'

Looking well satisfied with herself, Liza added, 'You go and see that nice Mr Wilson. See if you can persuade him to take more interest in you, dear. It shouldn't be difficult. Just let him know — subtly, you understand? — that you're interested. That'll be all it takes. You'll see!'

'Liza Tully!'

Anna fled before she could say anything else. No wonder the menfolk of the village all seemed to have thought Liza an entertainment when they were young. She wasn't much better even now, she thought with a rueful smile.

And what about Miss Fenwick? She didn't know what to think about that. Could it be true? A baby? Miss Fenwick? That was what Fred Baker had said, and now Liza had said it too. You had to wonder.

Such things used to happen, of course; and if the girl wasn't married, a baby would have been a bit of a scandal back then. Keeping quiet about it would have been very desirable from everyone's point of view — but it would have been hard to do in those days. In a little village like this, everyone would have known about such a thing, hush-hush or not. Disapproval wouldn't have been hard to find, either. Escaping the scandal could even be the reason why Miss Fenwick had left the village.

And now she was back.

How interesting. If it was true. And if it *was* true, what had happened to the child?

21

David woke up when she neared him.

'Oh, dear! I've done it again.'

'Done what?' he asked, yawning.

'Every time I go anywhere near someone who's asleep, they wake up. I'm so sorry, David. How are you feeling, anyway? Any better?'

'Much, much better, thank you! I really needed that. I was asleep on my feet.'

'I know,' she said with a smile. 'I saw you.'

'What about you, Anna? How are you?'

'I'm fine at the moment.'

He glanced at his watch. 'Heavens! Four o'clock? Is that really the time?'

'It could be.'

'I can't believe it. How is everybody? Anything changed?'

'No, I don't think so. Everything's

fine. You haven't missed anything.'

She held out a hand to help him get to his feet. Then, strangely, found herself unable to let go of his hand. Or was it that he couldn't let go of hers? She wasn't sure. Then, seemingly with embarrassment, they both let their hands drop, and stood gazing at each other sheepishly. She felt for a moment that he was going to kiss her, but he didn't.

'There is one new thing,' she said, trying to hide her awkwardness. 'Miss Fenwick. How much do you know about her?'

David shook his head. 'Next to nothing. Why?'

'I seem to have learned so much about her these past few hours. Did you know, for example, that she was — is — a professional artist? That it's how she has always made her living?'

'Nope. Never heard that.'

'Me neither. And do you know if she has family? Was she — is she — married, for example?'

'No idea. Where is this leading?'

'I'm not sure. Nowhere, probably,' she admitted. 'It's just that I've heard things tonight that surprised me. A couple of her contemporaries have said she used to go out with Willie McKenzie when they were young, for example. What do you think of that?'

David laughed. 'You've become a real gossipmonger, Anna! But carry on. What else have you learned?'

'Well, a couple of my confidantes reckon that Miss Fenwick — who, incidentally, is known here as Libby — had a baby at some point. If it's true, that would seem to put Willie McKenzie in the frame as the father.'

'Goodness me!' David chuckled. 'The old folks, eh? The things they used to get up to.'

'You're right. I'm beginning to see them all in a different light.'

'You would make a very good gossip columnist, Anna. Have you ever thought of working for one of the tabloids?'

'Actually, no. You have to admit, though, it is interesting, isn't it?' she said wistfully. 'I'm getting tired of hearing about nothing but rain and floods.'

David laughed. 'Come on, now. You lie down here and get some sleep. Let me take the graveyard watch.'

'Too late for that, David. It's already over. You have the four-till-eight watch now. It will give you the chance to see the dawn break.'

'And what will we see, I wonder, in the cold light of day?' David said with a grimace. 'I suspect it might be better to remain in the dark.'

Anna was inclined to agree, and she wasn't thinking only of the weather. She was wondering if what she had learned about Miss Fenwick might have been better never learned. Nobody would benefit if an ancient scandal — if that was what it was — came back to life. All the same, she had to admit she was intrigued. Who would have thought it?

Village life! she thought with a sigh,

before sleep claimed her for a little while. Their very own version of *Coronation Street* or *EastEnders*, right here in Carlton.

★   ★   ★

Soon after seven, the first greying of the darkness began. Standing outside the door of the church hall, Anna found she was starting to see things again. There were shapes all around her. Buildings and trees. Close by, there were humps representing vehicles that had been parked along the road, or washed there from somewhere else. Everywhere there was the sheen of the watery surface. The village, like Venice, occupied a lagoon now. Overhead, a few stars had appeared as the thick blanket of cloud had begun to thin. It was a new day in Carlton.

'What does it look like?' asked a voice beside her.

She turned, startled. 'Oh, good morning, Greg!'

'Anything good about it?'

'I don't know yet. We'll have to see. At least it's getting light.'

'Always a good sign. The rain has stopped, as well.'

'You're right. I hadn't even noticed.'

They stood and watched as grey light spread through the village. Anna was appalled by what it revealed. She couldn't believe how the place had been transformed.

'How will we ever get back to normal?' she wondered aloud, her usual confidence and optimism draining away as the magnitude of the task ahead of them became clearer.

'I have no idea,' Greg said. 'All I know is that we will. People always do. Somehow they recover from the worst that's thrown at them.'

'Thank you, Greg! That's the spirit. You've cheered me up no end.'

He chuckled. They stood there a little longer, watching as the light grew stronger. What a difference a night makes, Anna was thinking, and not only with regard to how the village looks. This man, who I hated yesterday, has been revealed to me as a very nice person!

'Have you seen disasters before?' she asked, thinking of what he had told her about his work and the places he had been.

'Yes, I have.' Greg nodded. 'I've seen a few disasters. And, believe me, this isn't one of them. I've seen floods that cost hundreds of lives, and earthquakes that cost a lot more. Viewed objectively, this is just a minor inconvenience in comparison.'

'Yes, you're right. That's all it is. We should remember that.'

What a different sort of life Greg led, she thought. He must have seen some rare sights.

'Have you travelled abroad a lot?'

'I suppose I have. It sometimes seems like everywhere they've ever wanted a new power station, I've been. The Middle East, the Gulf, mainly. But South America and India as well. Other places.'

'So home is where you hang your hat?'

'Pretty much.'

'It must be wonderful to have the chance to see so many countries. How I envy you! I did once go to France, on a school trip, but that was the only time I've ever been abroad.'

'Nowhere else?'

'Only Scotland. Does that count?'

Greg laughed. 'Not at the moment, no! Anyway, it's not all you might think, working abroad. It has its costs.'

She wondered if that was a reference to his failed marriage. Not every wife, or marriage, would cope well with frequent and perhaps lengthy absences by the husband. Poor Fiona was a good example of one who seemed to be tiring of it. But I'm sure it would suit me down to the ground, she reflected. I'm a little bored with going to the same old place every working day.

'Did you get any sleep?' Greg asked.

'Not really. I laid down for an hour

and got some rest. I may even have dozed a little, but that was all. Thankfully, David managed a couple of hours' sleep. He really needed it.'

'David Wilson?'

She nodded. 'He's had so much on his shoulders. He was absolutely exhausted. I found him in the corridor, asleep on his feet, sliding down the wall. I've never seen anything like it. I didn't even know it was possible.'

'It's not good to be like that.'

'No. You're right. He seems OK now, though. How about you, Greg? Did you get any sleep?'

He nodded. 'For a while. I found a nice, warm, quiet corner, and got my head down. I'm OK. Anything happen overnight? Did I miss anything?'

'Any births or deaths, you mean?' Anna said with a chuckle. 'No, nothing.'

'Not like the movies, then. No emergency surgery to be done by a George Clooney lookalike?'

Anna laughed. 'There's plenty of

time yet, Greg. Don't even joke about it, please!'

She thought for a moment, and then added, 'I had one or two intriguing conversations, though. Miss Fenwick, who we brought in last night . . . '

'What about her? She's all right, I assume?'

'Oh, yes. It's just that a couple of the older ones, people who knew her when they were all young, said she walked out — I think that was the phrase — with your grandfather. How about that?'

'Really?' Greg chuckled. 'Hard to imagine, isn't it? We'll have to pull his leg about that one.'

'I wonder if your grandmother knew?'

He grinned. 'Who knows?'

'Oh, it would have been long before she married Willie, anyway. What was she like, by the way, your grandmother?'

Greg shook his head. 'I don't remember her. I was just a baby when she died.'

'Mind you,' Anna said, reverting to the picture in her head of young Willie McKenzie and Libby Fenwick, 'knowing this village, and the old folk in it, 'walking out' together back then might have just meant that two people were seen one day walking on the same footpath.'

'In the same direction?' Greg suggested.

She laughed. 'Come on! Let's go back inside and see if anybody else is awake yet.'

22

People were stirring. David was back on the bridge of the ship once again, steering it through choppy waters. There were people to feed, and others to console and encourage. There were arrangements to be made and consultations to be held. Imminent arrivals to be planned for and accommodated.

'What's going on, David?' Anna asked.

'Things are moving, I'm happy to say. The Fire and Rescue Service say they will have a crew here within the hour. The police are coming with them. Our nurses are in touch with local doctors, and a couple of them will get here as soon as they can to check the people in poor health. Meanwhile, Doris and Mary are starting to cook breakfast.'

'All's well with the world?' Anna suggested.

'It is.'

'But it's a pity,' Greg suggested, 'that none of the public services came in during the night. Now is a bit late, isn't it?'

'Well, perhaps,' David admitted. 'But there were other villages not as well-prepared, or as resourceful, as ours. Probably worse affected, too. So we were not a priority. And we've managed, haven't we?'

So we have, Anna thought with a weary smile, as she turned away to see if anyone in the hall needed her help.

★ ★ ★

When she was called to the front door, Anna couldn't believe her eyes. Four men in a boat? Impossible. But it was!

She stared, incredulous, for a moment. Then she called out to them, 'Good morning!'

One of the men in the yellow dinghy stopped paddling for a moment. 'Morning, missus! We're looking for a flooded village. Have you seen one around here?'

'You've found it!' she said, laughing.

He made a performance of searching for it, hand over his eyes.

'Is there just you, or are there other rescuers on the way? We need more help than four men in a little boat can provide.'

The men all laughed, and began to paddle again. Their spokesman said, 'We're the advanced guard. Northumberland Fire and Rescue Service.'

The men steered the boat towards the front steps of the hall.

'Am I glad to see you!' Anna assured them. 'I'm just going to get the boss.'

She found him administering the preparation of breakfast. 'Help has arrived, David! The Fire and Rescue Service is here.'

He looked round and dropped tools. 'At last!' he said, beaming as he rushed to greet their visitors.

After that, things became a bit of a blur so far as Anna was concerned. The first arrivals were soon followed by others. More men from the Fire and Rescue Service, police officers and paramedics. Even men and women from the Mountain Rescue Team. They were all very good, too. Efficient and friendly, as if they had been doing this sort of thing all their lives.

A few people in the hall had not weathered the night very well, and those in need of medical attention were soon whisked away in a couple of boats with outboard engines. It was a relief to see them in good hands.

Some of the firefighters turned out to be very good at making porridge, and took their turn in the kitchen. Others moved on to search the village, having established that most people in the hall were basically in good shape.

The senior man from the rescue service, who said his name was Geoff Morgan, had a quick word with David and Anna.

'I'm sorry you've had to cope unaided overnight, but you've done a great job here. If only more villages and towns were as well-organised as you are!'

'Well, we did our best,' David said.

'A very good best! I'm afraid we couldn't get here any sooner. We had to establish priorities. Once you told us you could cope overnight, we had to concentrate on places that were in worse trouble.'

'How bad is it?' Anna asked.

'Bad enough,' he said with a grimace. 'People trapped in their cars. Whole villages underwater. Trees down, blocking access. Just getting around is problem enough. We could do with a fleet of helicopters.

'Anyway, the good news is that the flood has peaked. The water will steadily go down now. Later today, we'll have some pumps here. We'll get them working. They'll soon make a difference.'

'For the houses?' David asked.

Geoff shook his head. 'Not at first. The priority will be access and movement around the village by vehicle. We've got to have that before we can do much else.'

'What about people returning to their homes?' Anna asked.

'It's up to them. They'll want to see what's happened, of course, and maybe start salvaging things. But a lot of the houses underwater won't be habitable for a while. Some people are going to have to find somewhere else to stay for the time being.'

'There are a few guesthouses in the village,' Anna said, thinking about it.

'And lots of people will put their neighbours and friends up,' David added.

'There you are, then,' George said with a nod of approval. 'That's a good start right there.'

★ ★ ★

As the light grew stronger, so the water level began to fall. After an hour or two the difference was visible. A few people began to drift away then, heading back to their homes to assess the damage. Most, though, stayed where they were. They didn't have the boots and clothing for wading through the streets, and they were hungry and in need of hot food and a drink. The kitchen stayed busy.

Later that morning, Greg announced that he'd had a word with his grandfather, and was going to go to check his house over and see what could be done.

'He may not be able to go back there immediately,' Anna cautioned.

'He knows that. If he can't, I'll find somewhere for him to stay. We'll get it sorted.'

'Thanks, Greg!' she said, clutching his sleeve. 'I'm glad you're looking out for him. There'll be plenty of others for me to worry about.'

He smiled. 'I'm sure there will — and I can see you're good at worrying!'

'Oh, go away!' she said, laughing.

Liza Tully was one of the elderly who said she had family coming to collect her. If she couldn't get back into her own home, she would stay with them.

'In the village?'

'Just outside. My son has Crow's Nest Farm.'

'Up on the hill? Oh, you'll be all right there, Liza.'

'I don't know. It's a windy spot, you know?'

'Windy?' Anna laughed. 'That's better than watery, isn't it?'

'I'll let you know when I've been there a few days. I just hope I can get back into my own house soon.'

'Oh, you will. Don't worry about that. And I'll come when I can to help you sort things out.'

23

David was soon busy helping people who didn't have local family or friends to sort out alternative accommodation for them. Anna joined him. They set up in a small room he was using as an office and started working the phones. The guesthouse owners were the first port of call, and all half-dozen of them were eager to help.

After half an hour, Anna suddenly wondered how Miss Fenwick was. She hadn't caught sight of her for a while.

'I'm just going to find Miss Fenwick, David. I want to see if she's all right.'

David waved to acknowledge what she'd said, and continued his telephone discussion with a woman from what used to be called the water board, but which was now apparently some private company headquartered in Spain, of all places.

Miss Fenwick — or Libby, as Anna was starting to think of her — was sitting happily in the kitchen, eating porridge. She was in the midst of a group of young mums and their children. It was a relief to see her like that, seemingly enjoying the company, and at the same time making some of the children — the ones who were evidently not in awe of her — laugh at the caricatures she was drawing of them, sketched on scraps of paper with a pencil stub.

'Hello, Libby! How are you doing?'

'Good morning, Anna! I am perfectly well, thank you. Despite my misgivings, I managed to sleep a little, and this morning I feel fine. These ladies and their children are making me feel quite at home.'

'That's good. I'm glad you've found some company.'

'Oh, yes! Do you know, Anna, all these wonderful young people live in the village. I never knew that.'

Only because you never go out of

your house! Anna thought mischievously.

'And we've lived here all our lives, as well!' one of the mums said, laughing.

'So have I,' a five-year old boy assured Anna.

'Of course you have,' Anna responded. 'And so have I. I even went to school with your mum.'

That astonished the boy. He turned to his mother indignantly. 'You never said you went to school!'

Amid the laughter that followed, Libby squeezed Anna's hand affectionately. Goodness! Anna thought. We really must be feeling better.

★   ★   ★

Later, she happened to be present when Willie McKenzie met Libby for the first time in many a year.

'Libby! Is it really you, Libby? After all these years?'

Anna glanced round to see Willie coming towards them, a shy smile on

167

his face. Libby looked uncertain. Anna quickly moved in to help her out.

'Good morning, Willie McKenzie! You've woken up at last, have you?'

'I have,' he said, still smiling. 'But they tell me I kept everybody else awake most of the night with my snoring.'

'Not quite, but at one time I did wonder if we were having an earthquake as well as floods.'

Willie turned to Libby. 'They told me last night you were here, Libby. It's a good long time since I saw you, but you look wonderful — as pretty as ever!'

Anna's brief intervention had allowed Libby to recover, and to realise who it was that had spoken to her.

'Nonsense!' she said now. 'But you always were full of nonsense, Willie McKenzie. How are you, anyway? Enjoying all the excitement?'

'Huh! Is that what you call it? As a matter of fact,' he added with a twinkle in his eye, 'I am. The flood has made a bit of a welcome change!'

Anna was relieved that either Libby really did recognise him, or her own intervention had saved the day. She would have hated to see Willie facing the humiliation of not being remembered.

'I must get back to helping David,' she said. 'Can I leave you two to chat?'

'Of course you can!' Willie boomed. 'There's nothing I'd like better.'

For once, to Anna's relief, Libby didn't automatically reject what someone else had said. Nor did she seem annoyed to have been approached by Willie. Instead, her face wore a smile, suggesting she might even be amused. Anna seized the opportunity to make her escape and leave them to it.

24

It took a while — several weeks, in fact — for the village to return to anything like normal. Even then, there were plenty of dwellings that were still unfit to be reoccupied. Sunnyside House was just one of them, but it was one that attracted a lot of attention from Anna. She was sad to see such a magnificent house so forlorn and deserted. Someone had to look out for it, she felt.

Another reason was that she longed to see Miss Fenwick back there again, and painting once more. A guesthouse was no place for a person like her to live, in what was coming to seem like perpetuity. She needed to be back home — as, indeed, everyone else did.

A quite separate matter was Anna's fascination with the bits and pieces she had picked up about the early lives of some of the village's elderly citizens.

There were connections between them that she found quite fascinating. It was as if she had been handed a jigsaw puzzle that someone else had started and then abandoned. Now she had all sorts of pieces, and she had to find where they fitted. It wasn't easy.

The pieces that so perplexed her were actually questions, a series of questions. For example, did Libby really have a baby? And if she did, what happened to it? Had the child stayed here when Libby went, or was sent, away? If so, what had happened to it subsequently? Had the child become an adult who left the village, or was that person still here?

Questions, questions! she thought wryly. But someone must know the answers to them, and she would love to find out.

Anna's own cottage had pretty well escaped damage from the storm and the floods. A few tiles had come loose, the satellite dish was hanging by a thread — and quite useless — and there was a suggestion of wetness and damp in the wall of the living room that hadn't been there before, but overall she couldn't believe how lucky she had been. These things were as nothing at all. Yet other people, far less able to cope, had experienced terrible losses.

Some were expecting to be out of their homes for anything up to a year. In those cases, it wasn't just the visible damage that had been experienced. It was also that inundation by foul water had made the properties a health risk. The public health authorities and insurance companies had given stern warnings against reoccupation before walls, floors and everything else had been professionally cleaned, repaired, and then allowed to dry, a process that was expected to take many, many months.

In a way, Willie McKenzie was one of the lucky ones. The ground floor of his house had been swamped, but Greg had dealt with it, displaying his professional powers of organisation and know-how. A cleaning firm with lots of staff was brought in, along with plumbers and electricians. Huge industrial dehumidifiers were installed to work 24/7 once electricity was restored to the village. Then came kitchen fitters and carpet layers. In three weeks the house was habitable again, and Willie moved back in. By then, Greg was gone. Some foreign country that needed a power station built, Anna assumed, had claimed him once more.

'However did he manage it all?' Anna asked, when she came to visit Willie in his restored home.

'No idea,' Willie said, shaking his head, mystified. 'He's a good lad, though. Good at what he does.'

'And good to you, too,' Anna pointed out.

'Yes. I'll have to be careful what I say about him from now on,' Willie admitted with a grin.

'Me, too.' Anna paused uncertainly, and then said, 'How will it all be paid for? Do you know?'

'It's on the insurance. That's what Gregory said. It's all on them.'

Anna hoped that was right. Thousands must have been spent here, and Willie's pension wouldn't cover much of it. That was for sure.

'Well, I'm very pleased to see you back home again, Willie. There's no place like home, is there?'

Willie nodded agreement.

'I'll be getting along now,' Anna said. 'I want to call on Liza Tully. Her house wasn't too bad, and she hopes to be back in it soon. Miss Fenwick's house is a different matter, though. It's going to be a long time before she'll be able to move back in.'

Willie's head jerked round. 'Libby? Where's she now?'

'In the *Dunroamin* guesthouse still.'

'Is she all right?'

'I think so. As well as can be expected, anyway. I daresay she's bored and frustrated, not being in her own place, but there you are.

'I expect the two of you had a lot to

talk about when you met in the church hall, did you?' she added, curious about their meeting.

'Oh, aye. We did that.'

'Old times?'

'Old times,' he agreed, looking a little sad. 'She was a lovely girl, you know, Libby. Beautiful, and full of life. Very clever, as well.'

Anna nodded.

'She's an artist, you know?'

'Yes. She told me. Quite a career she's had, apparently.'

'I always thought she would do well. You could see that when we were young. She was far too good for the likes of me — or Fred Baker either!' Willie added with a grin. 'He was always trying to catch her eye. Not that it did him much good! Well,' he added, reflecting, 'not that I noticed. It didn't seem to.'

'Whatever do you mean, Willie?'

He smiled. 'We were sweethearts, Libby and me, when we were young. What were we? Fourteen or fifteen, maybe. Something like that. Too young to do anything about it, anyway. That was before I met Betty, mind. A long time before. Libby was away and gone by then.'

Gazing into the past, Willie reflected, 'It near broke my heart at the time, when she left. And I never saw her again until now. Funny, isn't it, how things work out? I'm glad I've seen her once more, though. I am.'

Anna suspected there was a tear in the corner of Willie's eye. Eager to avoid that, she said, 'Something good came from the flood, then?'

'Aye, it did!'

'So Libby left here when she was still a young girl?'

'Oh, yes! She did. Just up and away suddenly. I never knew what happened, or where she went either. Never heard from her again. Not once.'

'How sad. It must have been very upsetting for you. And you didn't know why she left?'

Willie straightened up and shook his

head. Anna got the distinct impression that he wouldn't say any more. His lips were sealed. He knew, she thought, but he wasn't going to say.

'Put the kettle on, pet,' Willie said gravely. 'Let's have a cup of tea. You'll have to make it, though. I haven't studied that new kettle Gregory got me yet.'

'Perhaps you have to put water in it, and then switch it on, Willie? What do you think?'

He stared at her a moment. Then he laughed and shook his head. 'Aye,' he said. 'That sounds about right!'

25

Anna thought the way Libby had left the village seemed strange, very strange. She had just been a young girl then, a teenager. She hadn't even been of an age when youngsters went off to college. Besides, it seemed to have been very sudden and unexpected, certainly so far as youngsters who knew her had been concerned.

Poor Willie! Anna thought with a wry smile. Young lovers torn apart. What heartbreak!

And what about Libby? Had she been just as upset? Perhaps. Somehow, though, Anna suspected not. Probably not at all, in fact. Libby was made of sterner stuff. She wouldn't have been so bothered, and she would certainly have recovered sooner.

Then there was Fred, who even now seemed to resent her. Was that because he had lost out to Willie in their rivalry for the young Libby's affections? Still carrying a grudge, after all this time?

It seemed unlikely. Besides, Fred's resentment didn't seem to be directed at Willie at all. It was at Libby herself. And, unlike Willie, he hadn't been in the least interested in meeting her again. Perhaps he had simply never really liked her — despite what Willie had said — and still didn't? After all, Libby had grown up with privilege, living in a big house with parents who had money. Not everyone would have appreciated that.

The more she thought about it, the more Anna came to believe there must be some truth in what she had heard when sealed lips had temporarily been unsealed. Had Libby really managed to get herself pregnant? she wondered with a smile.

Both Liza and Fred had spoken of her having had a baby. Surely they wouldn't both have made that up? It had to be true. Was that why she had suddenly disappeared, never to be seen in the village again until now?

An illegitimate birth would have been a serious matter in those days, a scandal of the first order, especially for a well-off, middle-class family. Such a family might well have decided the best thing to do was ship the errant girl off somewhere. Either to a distant part of the family or to a convent. From what Anna had read, they had been the usual options.

Containing the disgrace, as it was seen to be, would have been the priority, even over the welfare and interests of the girl and her baby. Correction: separating girl and baby would have been thought the best thing to do in both their interests. They didn't mess about in those days!

Anna frowned. Was that how it had been? Had she stumbled upon the explanation? If it was true, and Libby had brought a child into the world, who had been the father? Well, on the basis of what she had heard, it was hard to look past Willie McKenzie.

And what were the implications of that?

One was that Willie had fathered a child he had never seen. Another was that the legitimate son Willie and his wife had brought into the world would have had a half-sibling that he didn't know about either.

And that, of course, meant that Greg might have a . . . a what? A great-cousin? One he didn't know about? Well, it would be no good asking him about that!

Oh, it was impossible. She shook her head and gave a rueful smile. The ramifications, the possibilities, down the generations were far too complicated. They were doing her head in! Besides, what business was it of hers?

Forget about it, she told herself. It had all been a long time ago, anyway.

A more important, and more immediate, question was: would she ever see Greg again? She had expected to see something of him once the floodwater drained away, but she hadn't. He had worked like a Trojan sorting out his grandfather's house. Then he had disappeared, departed unannounced to a destination unknown.

She shrugged. Maybe he would turn up again. Maybe he would remember his suggestion that she should visit him in Newcastle. Probably not, though. Not a man like Greg.

She had helped him through a difficult night; and, to be fair, he had helped her too. But that was all it had been. Just one of those things. Like two people who for a time feel close to each other on an overnight train journey or sea crossing. *Close Encounter* all over again? Something like that. It was the way of the world.

26

Libby was doing all right in the guesthouse. She was bored, of course, and frustrated, and impatient at not being able to access her own things and her own space, but she was coping well enough. Anna had taken to visiting her most days, and taking in the little things she needed. She needed medication, of course, like most of the other older members of the community, although she was one of those who liked to pretend it was unnecessary. Anna sympathised. She wouldn't have wanted everybody in the village to know there was anything wrong with her either.

But Libby seemed to have taken to her. She was prepared to confide in her things that perhaps she wouldn't in others. There was no way she would have asked anyone in the guesthouse to obtain and deliver medicines and pills for her, but she seemed to have no compunction in asking Anna.

'It's your personality,' David said with a smile, 'your warm, friendly nature. She must feel she can ask you anything.'

'Thank you, David! I feel honoured. Just as long as I still have time to go to work, as well as collect things for people, I shan't mind.'

He nodded with understanding. 'Yes, of course. You do so much for so many people, don't you? I know that.'

'Not really. Just this and that, for those who look to me as their elder. Libby is the exception in that respect.'

'Well, don't let her lean too much on you. There are others who are prepared to help, remember.'

'David, please. No lectures! I'm well able to sort things out for myself.'

'Of course you are. What have you got there?'

'Just a few things.'

'Who for? You?'

'No, no. Just some sketching pads and pencils.'

'For?'

'Libby, of course. She's an artist, a working artist who is a bit frustrated just now because she can't work. I thought these might give her something to do.'

'I rest my case,' David said sternly.

Anna smiled. 'Actually, David, there's something I've been meaning to ask you to help me with. I want to go back to Sunnyside House and see what progress has been made there, if any. Would you come with me?'

'Of course. When do you want to go?'

'Sometime soon. It's Saturday tomorrow. How about tomorrow morning?'

David hunted through the diary in his memory bank before responding. 'Fine. Let's do that. Ten o'clock suit you?'

'Perfect. When I go to see Libby this evening, I'll tell her. She'll be pleased. And it will make me feel less guilty about having so little positive news for her.'

'Oh, don't ever let yourself feel guilty, Anna. You spend so much time doing things for others, there's no reason at all for you ever to feel like that.'

'Look who's talking!' she teased.

He grinned. 'Go on, get out of here! Let me get on with some work.'

'See you tomorrow, David.'

He smiled, held the door open for her, and waved her goodbye.

★ ★ ★

'You're very kind,' Libby said, when she saw what Anna had brought her. 'Just what I need! However did you think of it?'

'A working artist needs to work, Libby. Even I can appreciate that. And I can see how difficult it must be for you to be cooped up here. You don't complain — not very much! — but it must be frustrating for you.'

Libby laughed at herself. 'I suppose I

am terribly ungrateful. I always have been. I know that. Sometimes I wonder why. I had a privileged background and upbringing, and my life has been very rewarding ever since. Nothing to complain about at all, really.'

'Were you the only child in the village in that position, Libby? From a well-off home, I mean?'

The old lady reflected. 'Possibly I was. At least, I can't think of too many others. There were one or two children who were sent away to boarding schools. Not posh ones. Nothing like that. A popular choice was the Quaker school in York, I seem to recall.'

'Is that where you went when you left the village?'

'Oh, no! Nothing like that.'

Libby had ducked the question about what had happened to her, and now she seemed intent on diverting attention from it.

'Has the rain finished, do you think?' she asked.

'For now, I believe it has.'

Anna wanted to try one more probe before she gave up for the evening. 'Of course,' she said, 'children like Liza Tully and Willie McKenzie, and Fred Baker, all from working families, would just have stayed on at the village school, I suppose?'

'Yes. They did. That was the normal thing to do.'

Anna smiled. 'It's lovely to think of you all back then, when you were all youngsters. And it must have been fun for you to talk to them again that night when we were all together in the church hall. I gather it had been a long time since you had last seen them?'

'A very long time. And, yes, it was good to see them again, I suppose.' Libby considered, and then added, 'Not that we have so very much in common now. Just the memory of our early years, I suppose.'

'You didn't stay in touch — with Willie, say?'

Libby shook her head. 'Why would I?'

Anna shrugged and changed the subject, saying she intended visiting Sunnyside House again in the morning, and that David Wilson had kindly agreed to go with her. They would see how things were there, and come back to let her know. Understandably, Libby was pleased.

So that was that, Anna thought with a sigh afterwards. Getting information out of Libby was like trying to squeeze blood out of a stone.

27

Later, as she came away from the guesthouse, Anna thought what a poor interrogator she made. She had got next to nothing out of Libby. The old lady had sidestepped all her leading questions and insinuations, seemingly without any effort at all. Her dodging of the notion that she might have stayed in contact with Willie McKenzie had been particularly adroit.

Was it possible to feel you had nothing in common with someone who had been, or might have been, the father of your child? Perhaps it was, if you were a singularly selfish and egocentric person. Was that what Libby was? Well, yes. Possibly. Probably, in fact.

All the same, even if you were that way, if you returned to the village where you had been born and raised, after most of a lifetime away, would you not have more interest in your former lover? And would you have nothing to say about the child the two of you had brought into the world?

And so, on and on, it went. It was so frustrating. She really ought to give it up, this searching after answers to ancient questions that were none of her business.

Not feeling quite ready to go home yet, she decided to visit another of her wards: Liza Tully, who was now back in her own home.

'I can't tell you how pleased I am to be back,' Liza said as soon as she saw Anna.

'I just bet you are. Willie McKenzie says the same thing. And plenty of others are also back in their own homes. I wish I could say the same about Fred Baker, but he's one of the unlucky ones, I'm afraid. His house needs a lot more work, and time, spending on it.'

Liza shook her head. 'Fred always

was unlucky. If there was a short straw on offer, Fred would be the one to grab it.'

Anna smiled. 'I'm not sure about that, Liza. He doesn't seem unlucky to me. He seems to have had a life of contentment, and to have been very happy with his wife for many, many years.'

'Probably,' Liza said with a sniff. 'Eventually, perhaps.'

'Dear Liza, whatever do you mean? No!' Anna said, laughing. 'Don't tell me. I don't want to know. I only want to hear good things about people today.'

'That's you all over,' Liza said. 'It's the same with David Wilson. You only want to know good things, both of you. Well, let me tell you . . . '

Anna put her hands over her ears.

'All right,' Liza said with a grin, relenting. 'I'll stop.'

'Good. Now, how are you getting on? Everything sorted?'

'Yes, I think so. The new carpet in the

hall is nice, isn't it?'

'It is. Did you choose it?'

'Yes. My daughter brought me a pattern book, and I chose it from there.'

'Your family has done very well, getting everything sorted for you. Gregory McKenzie has done the same for Willie. Someone I'm worried about, though, is Miss Fenwick. She hasn't got any family to support her. David and I are doing our best, but we don't have the time for everything she needs.'

'Oh, you needn't worry about her. She'll be all right. Libby has plenty of money.'

Anna chuckled. 'Money won't get the water out of her house, Liza! It won't find carpets and wallpaper for her either. It's just such a pity she doesn't have any family to sort things out for her.'

'Her daughter will probably do that for her. She'll be all right.'

'She doesn't have a daughter, Liza. She never married.'

'She might not ever have married,

but she has a daughter,' Liza said stubbornly. 'We weren't supposed to know about it, but we all do.'

'Who does? What does that mean?'

'Well, the family tried to hush it up when Libby got pregnant, but it was known in the village. Everybody knew. She had a little girl. Then she was sent away, with the baby. To some relatives down south, I heard.'

Not exactly proof, Anna thought, but it was something more. Bit by bit, she seemed to be learning more. What Liza had just said sounded right.

'And mother and daughter were never seen again?'

'Well, Libby wasn't, not until she came back a couple of years ago, but the daughter was.'

'Oh?'

'She used to come to stay with her grandparents during the school holidays, when she was little. I don't know what happened to her when she grew up. But if Libby doesn't know, she should do!'

Anna was inclined to agree.

'But that was Libby all over,' Liza said sadly. 'She always was out for herself. Don't get me wrong. She was very clever, and bonny, but other people didn't matter much to her.

'Mind you, I can't blame her family for sending her away. That's what used to happen in them days. They must have been furious with her — not that Libby would have been very bothered about that.'

'So what happened to Willie?'

'Willie?'

'Willie McKenzie. I assume he was the father?'

Liza smiled and shook her head. 'You'll have to ask him, pet! I couldn't tell you. That's one thing I don't know.'

28

Anna walked down into the village, and together she and David walked up to Sunnyside House, partly for the exercise, and partly because David had not tried to start his car since the flood, and doubted if he could now.

'Time for a new one, David?' Anna suggested.

'I'll have to see how much I've got in the piggy bank,' he told her with a grin.

But it was a lovely morning, and neither of them minded walking.

'All week I sit on a chair,' Anna said. 'I'm happy to rediscover my feet at the weekend.'

'I know what you mean. I don't get out much during the week either. I'm thinking of having the phone taken out of the office. That might help.'

Anna laughed. She was happy. The village was slowly returning to normal and her own life was back on an even keel. And here she was, on a Saturday morning in good company.

For the moment, at least, she had almost forgotten that she was working out her notice, and would soon be scrabbling around looking for another job.

'You've been up to the house a couple of times already, haven't you?' David said. 'What are you expecting to find today?'

'I'm not sure. The other day the downstairs was still flooded, but I'm hoping the water will have drained away by now. If it hasn't, maybe we could get somebody in with a pump.'

'The Environment Agency,' David said thoughtfully. 'They're the people to contact. We have pumps back at the yard, but they're just small ones. We'll get the professionals in to do the job. They've been pumping out plenty of other houses lately.'

Anna felt thankful she had asked David to come with her today. She had been doing her best, but she didn't know how these things worked. Because of his job, David did. Perhaps after this visit she would have something more positive to tell Libby.

'It's just the downstairs, I take it?' David said.

'So far as I know. I haven't been upstairs since we rescued Libby. The upstairs was OK then, though.'

'We'll have a good look round.'

'Oh, something else! There's a window Greg and I had to break to get into the house.'

'I'll get one of the lads from the yard to come up to fix that. What about your little house? Everything all right there?'

'It seems to be. I was lucky.'

'Luckier than me. My kitchen was flooded.'

'Oh, David! You didn't say. How are you managing?'

'The same as everybody else,' he said with a grin. 'I've added myself to the list of people I pray for!'

The front garden of Sunnyside House was still a lake. It didn't look good, Anna thought, as they stood for a moment gazing across it.

'There can't be any drainage,' David said, puzzled. 'That wants seeing to. If the water can't drain away itself, it'll be here till it evaporates next summer.'

'If it's a good summer,' Anna suggested.

'That's a point. Come on! Let's see what the house is like.'

Not much different, was Anna's first impression when she opened the front door with the key Libby had given her. There was still water sloshing around the hall and the kitchen, although the level was perhaps a little lower now.

'Oh, this is no good at all,' David said, shaking his head. 'We'll get somebody in to pump the water out.'

With that, he fished out his mobile phone and made a call. Anna wandered on when he started talking to someone about the problem. Thank goodness David was here, she thought again. He knew how to do these things, and who to contact. He was also so good at actually getting them done. He had the energy, and the drive.

In the kitchen, her eyes flew to the pictures on the walls. Libby's paintings. She was very pleased to see they were untouched by the disaster that had overtaken the house. She closed her eyes for a moment in appreciation, and gave a satisfied smile.

Really, she didn't care about the fridge and the washing machine, the freezer and the tumble drier. They could all be replaced. And the old oak table would be unaffected even if it stood in water for a century or more. But she would have hated to see Libby's paintings go under.

She turned, still smiling, as David stopped speaking on the phone, and she heard him coming sloshing in from the hall.

'It's a bit wet in here as well, isn't it?'

he said, looking around.

'Just a bit.'

'Well, the Environment Agency guy promised to get a crew up here today — this morning, hopefully. They'll soon pump this lot out.'

'Thank you, David. Libby will be so pleased when I tell her something is being done at last.'

'This the art collection?' David asked, running his eyes around the walls.

'A small part of it, I think.'

'They're very good, aren't they? Just what you want to see when you get up on a dull cloudy day in Northumberland.'

Anna laughed and agreed.

'Reminds me of my mother's house,' David said.

'Oh? Does she paint?'

'She does. Paints and draws. Pictures all over the place. When I used to arrive home from primary school, there was never anywhere left to stick the masterpieces I'd produced.'

'Poor David!'

He looked sorrowful for a moment, then added, 'So I decided to concentrate on playing football.'

'Probably more money in football?'

'Not that I ever found.'

'More fun, then?'

'Definitely.'

Strange, she thought. I can't recall David speaking of his mother before. All the years I've known him, as well. How odd.

'Where does your mother live, David? Still in Nether Edge?'

That was a neighbouring, but much smaller, village. She knew David had lived there as a boy. He had come to school here, but hadn't arrived to live in Carlton until some years after he started working in the builder's yard, when it was run by Micky's father.

'Still there,' he agreed.

'Do you know, David, I can't recall ever seeing your mother.'

'No? She lives a quiet life, I suppose. Doesn't come here very often at all. She goes to Alnwick for her shopping.'

'Bigger shops, more choice?'

'I suppose so.' He hesitated. 'I don't know why, or even if it's true, but I've always felt she doesn't like Carlton. She's always seemed to avoid it, if at all possible.'

Anna shrugged. 'We all have our preferences.'

'True,' he said with a nod. 'Come on! Let's see what the rest of the house is like.'

29

The whole of the ground floor was flooded still. Every room, and every nook and cranny. The pantry, the cupboards — everywhere! David tut-tutted as they looked behind every door, and then he pored over the broken window.

'I'll soon get that fixed,' he said. 'The window isn't a conventional modern size, but we've got glass we can cut.'

Defensively, Anna said, 'I should have done more, I know. But my focus has been on people, David. I've been trying to make sure those I'm responsible for looking after are OK, as well as going to work. I just couldn't take time off . . .'

'Just stop it, Anna!' David smiled at her and shook his head. 'You're a wonder, Anna. You really are! You've done extraordinarily well by everybody.

We all know how much you've been doing.'

She relaxed. She knew he meant it. It wasn't what her mother would call 'flannel'. It was sincere.

She smiled. 'I just didn't want you to wonder why I haven't done anything about this house. That's all.'

'Anna,' he said sternly, 'Miss Fenwick, and her house, are not something we are responsible for. Get that out of your head. We help as much as we can, but there's a limit to what we can do.'

'I just didn't want you to think . . . '

'I know what you're about to say! But I have nothing but praise for what you've been doing these past weeks. Nobody else has, either. Frankly, I couldn't have managed to keep going myself without your support. Your cheerfulness and unfailing energy have kept me and everybody else chugging along. Think on that!'

She gave him a wan smile. 'Thank you, David. It's very kind of you to say such things.'

'I mean them, too.'

She nodded. Then she looked around the big drawing room, waved her arms and said, 'It's just that I wish I had been able to do more about Libby's house. I do like her, you know?'

David chuckled. 'She's a mean, waspish old thing. But I like her, too. She's a character, and she is likeable in a roguish sort of way, isn't she? Well, we'll sort her house out for her, and get her back home as soon as we possibly can.'

'Thank you, David.' Anna smiled at him with gratitude. 'I couldn't do it all myself, but the two of us together can. Now, let's look upstairs. There's something up there that I would particularly like you to see.'

There were six bedrooms on the upper floor, and two bathrooms. The master bedroom was en-suite.

'Goodness!' David said, 'Keeping everybody clean must have been a big thing in the olden days. I never would have thought it.'

'What? You thought that in big houses like this there would be a tin bath hanging on a nail in the outhouse? They would bring it in three times a year and fill it with hot water?'

'Something like that,' David said, chuckling. 'And all these bedrooms! Doesn't Miss Fenwick rattle around the house a bit?'

'I would imagine she does, but I don't really know. I haven't been here in normal circumstances. Anyway, she's happy here. That's the main thing, isn't it?'

'Indeed it is. She probably just lives in part of the house anyway.'

Anna nodded. 'That's what I thought. It would make sense. But you still haven't seen all the house yet.'

'Oh? What have I missed?'

'Come on! I'll show you.'

Anna led the way to the end of the landing and opened a door that might have been the entrance to a linen cupboard, but wasn't. A narrow stair-case was revealed. She led the way up it, and into a long attic with big skylight windows set in the sloping roof.

'This seems to be the studio where Libby works,' Anna said, waving around at an extraordinary clutter of easels, brimming shelves and cupboards, collections of bric-a-brac, and countless photographs of landscapes and wildlife.

'She'd need good light, but not direct sunshine, I would imagine. So this northerly side of the house would be ideal.'

'I see what you mean. So she really is an artist?'

'Yes. She is. I've looked her up on the internet, and she's quite well-known. Famous, really.'

'Goodness!'

They stood and looked for a minute or two, taking in the scene, but without touching anything.

'And through here,' Anna said, turning to a door set in the wall that ran the length of the attic, 'is what seems to be her gallery.'

She opened the door and led the way

into a parallel room on the other side of the house.

'No skylights here,' David said, glancing up at the ceiling.

'No. Just the two small windows, and they have heavy blinds drawn over them. Presumably that's to stop light damaging the paintings.'

David fingered a panel of switches and began turning on lights that illuminated individual paintings on the walls.

'Such a lot,' he murmured, impressed.

'Yes. And even more stored in racks at the far end of the room, and in another room beyond.'

David shook his head in amazement. 'I thought Mum had a lot of paintings, but she has nothing like this collection.'

'Does your mother sell her work?'

'I don't think so. Maybe an occasional piece. It's just a hobby for her, really.'

'It's not for Libby. This, I believe, is her life's work. It's why she was put on earth. Looking at this, all this wonderful creative outpouring, I feel we can forgive her all sorts of personal failings.'

'Not ours to forgive, Anna. But I know what you mean.'

They gazed around for a couple more minutes. Then David said, 'Come on! I've seen enough. We have work to do.'

30

'How did you get on with Miss Fenwick?' David asked.

Anna smiled ruefully. 'All right, I suppose. But what a strange person she is. She's far too complicated for me to deal with. I never know where I stand, unless we're talking about practical matters.'

'Speaking of which?'

'Oh, yes! She's OK with everything we're doing, and grateful for it. Yes, we can scrap the electrical appliances, as they can be replaced on the insurance, but we are to keep carpets, rugs and furniture — for now, at least. Some of that stuff is unusual, rare even, and suitably valuable. Libby will consult a friend of hers who specialises in textile restoration, and no doubt another friend who is an expert on furniture. She seems to have lots of friends of that sort. It's just a pity they haven't turned up to help her in her hour of need.'

'Try not to be cynical, dear!' David advised with a grin.

She pulled a face. 'Very well. I'll try.'

'Good.' David yawned and stretched. 'We'll get on with things, then.'

'How did you manage, David?'

'Well, I just let the Environment Agency men into the house, and left them to it. They thought they could have the water pumped out by the end of the day. After that, the drying and cleaning can start. Likely to be a long job, I think.'

'Well, we've made a start.'

'Yes, you're right.' He glanced at his watch and added, 'Come on! Lunch-time.'

* * *

The King's Head was a fine old country pub, an historic coaching inn, in fact, that had been in business for several centuries. It had long since lost its role on the country's major passenger transport artery, but visitors and tourists helped to keep it going as a pub with a fine culinary tradition. It was one of the few places in the area where a traveller could get a meal at any time, from early morning to late at night. The lunch trade, especially on a weekend, was always busy, but they managed to get a table with a fine view of the nearby hills.

'I'm ready for this,' David announced with relish.

'Hungry?'

'I'll say!'

She smiled. As it happened, she wasn't hungry, but she was enjoying the occasion. Eating out was a rare event for her.

'This your regular hostelry, David?'

He shook his head. 'I don't get out very often, certainly not as often as I would like to.'

'Too busy?'

'Well . . . There is that, of course, but it's also the case that dining out alone can be a miserable experience.'

'Alone? You? Surely not?'

'What? You think I lead a wild social life?'

'No. Of course I don't. But I'm sure you have loads of friends to go out with.'

'Not so many that I can persuade to go out at a moment's notice. Most have wives, partners, or girlfriends, and quite rightly they have to put them and their families first. Oh, I do go out occasionally with friends, but it tends to be on outings organised well in advance. How about you?'

She dodged the question, unwilling to admit what a limited social life she led.

'Oh, you know. Girls from work. We get together from time to time to do something special, and that always involves a meal at some point.'

'In town?'

She nodded.

'Working in a bigger place must make a difference. Here, all I see all day are harassed men from the building trade — plus Micky's charming face!'

'Now who's being cynical?'

He laughed and wagged a finger at her. '*Touché!*'

'Well,' Anna said quietly, 'I can tell you I'm enjoying this lunch opportunity. Thank you for asking me, David.'

'You're very welcome. I'm enjoying it, too,' he said with a smile. 'Oh, here comes our food. My, they have been quick!'

They dawdled over their meal, and afterwards had a second cup of coffee.

'I've really enjoyed our lunch,' David said shyly. 'I've wanted to do something like this for a long time. We see each other at church and at meetings, and we do things together for other people, but how often do we have the chance and the time to talk together? Not often, do we?'

Anna smiled. 'It's true. You're so busy, David.'

'Me? What about you?'

'I don't do half what you do.'

'Only because your job takes you out of the village every day, whereas I'm here all the time.'

'Perhaps.'

'I was wondering,' David said, looking serious. 'Are you happy with your life, and the way things are going?'

'Of course I am!' she replied with a chuckle. 'Not a thing to complain about at all. I have a house, a job, friends. I live where I am happy living, and I have lots to keep me busy. Why do you ask?'

He shrugged and smiled. 'Just wondering. Nothing else you want to do, or to have?'

'Oh, I wouldn't say that, exactly! There's always something, isn't there? I suppose, if you twisted my arm, I would admit to a hidden fancy for some foreign travel, for seeing a bit more of the world.'

'Is there no chance of that?'

'Well . . . ' Suddenly she recalled her conversations with Greg. Their words had seemed to offer a small possibility of realising that dream — if they ever saw each other again. 'I wouldn't say that, exactly either. But I have no plans at the moment. How about you, and your life?'

'I'm very happy, too,' he said brightly. 'I couldn't wish for anything else.'

'How lucky we are, then,' she said with a smile.

'Yes, aren't we?' David responded, but somehow she wasn't sure she believed him, any more than she believed what she had said herself.

* * *

David paid for the meal with a card. As he stuffed the receipt into his wallet, he hesitated a moment and then said, 'I've an idea. You said you'd never met my mother. Why don't we make a day of it, and go and see her?'

She frowned, unsure. 'Really? Do you want to do that?'

'I wouldn't have suggested it if I didn't.'

'Is she expecting you? I wouldn't

want to inconvenience or embarrass her.'

'Don't worry about that. She's always complaining that she never sees me. She'll be delighted to be visited. What do you say?'

Anna shrugged. 'OK. That sounds nice. Let's do it. How will we get there, though?'

David frowned. He hadn't thought of that. Glancing out of the window, he said, 'I see the sun's shining. Maybe my car will start at last?'

Anna laughed. 'Is it really worth trying?'

'I don't know. Maybe.'

David's qualified optimism was justified. The Volvo did start. He revved the engine briskly and told her to jump in before it stalled.

'Let's go!' he cried. 'The run will do it the world of good.'

And me too, Anna thought, laughing. What a day she was having!

31

The home in which David had grown up was a delightful little stone cottage, surrounded by an extensive garden. As they pulled into the short drive, Anna could see a big lawn studded with fruit trees, a beech hedge to act as a windbreak, herbaceous flower beds, and a well-kept kitchen garden shielded by an old stone wall. She had the impression that the garden was very well-maintained, even in winter.

'What a lovely place,' she commented as they got out of the car. 'Your mother must be a keen gardener.'

'She always has been,' David acknowledged. 'She grows things for the summer shows, and always wins prizes for her sweet peas and flower displays.'

The front door opened as they approached. We've been spotted! Anna thought with a nervous smile. I do hope it's all right, arriving unexpectedly like this.

A middle-aged woman wearing trousers, a roll-neck jumper, a padded gilet and a big smile stepped outside.

'Hi, Mum!' David called. 'Glad we've caught you in.'

'Oh, you'll usually catch me in these days! Hello, David. I was just going to do some clearing-up in the garden. But come on inside. I'll put the kettle on.'

David introduced Anna.

'I'm pleased to meet you, Mrs Wilson.'

'Hello, dear. I must thank you for bringing David to see me. It doesn't happen anywhere near enough. I scarcely see him from one month to the next.'

'Total exaggeration, of course!' David protested.

Anna laughed and began to relax. Already she sensed she would like David's mother. She seemed a warm, friendly person.

The conversation flowed very easily. David and his mother were both charming, both to Anna and to each other. Anna found herself thinking David must have had a happy childhood.

'This is a lovely cottage, Mrs Wilson. Have you always lived here?'

'Oh, no! But I have been here a long time, I suppose. David and I came to live here when he was just a toddler. Before that, we lived in London.'

'That was a big leap to come all this way, back in those days,' Anna said with surprise.

'Not so big for me, actually. My grandparents lived in Carlton when I was young, and I used to visit them often in school holidays. So I knew the area, and always liked it. After my husband died when David was still very young, I decided moving here would be good for us both.'

'And you never changed your mind?'

Mrs Wilson shook her head. 'I rented this cottage initially, and later I bought it. As much as anything, it was the garden that attracted me. I could see myself as the new Capability Brown!'

David snorted with amusement. 'Mother, I really don't believe Capability Brown would have bothered with Brussels sprouts and leeks.'

'Perhaps not,' Mrs Wilson conceded. 'But every gardener must start somewhere. In any case, I'm sure Mr Brown didn't always plant nothing but trees.'

'You never wanted to move over to Carlton, like David?' Anna asked.

'No. He had to get on with his life, and I've been very happy here. Besides, where would I find a better garden? Oh, I'm just an old stick-in-the-mud!'

David said, 'I have encouraged Mother to help me tend the plants in containers in my backyard, but she doesn't seem terribly interested.'

'David,' Anna said sternly, 'if there ever were plants in those containers, I've never seen them. Anyway, by now they will have been washed away in the floods.'

'True enough,' he conceded.

'Are things getting back to normal in Carlton now?' Mrs Wilson asked.

'Gradually,' Anna said. 'But there are still a few people who will be unable to return to their homes for some time yet.'

'You must all have had a terrible time. We were lucky here. The river behaved itself.'

'Things would have been much worse for people,' Anna said, 'if the village hadn't had David to organise the rescue and recovery operation. He's been wonderful.'

'So I hear. And you, too, Anna. People say the pair of you made such a difference.'

Anna shrugged. 'I just tried to help. It was David who carried the burden.'

'Nonsense!' David said quietly. 'Mother, this insufferably modest young woman was positively heroic. We would have been in trouble without her.'

'David, I can't let you say such things!'

With a smile, Mrs Wilson patted her hand gently. 'From what I hear,' she said, 'David is quite right. Thank you for helping him, and for doing so much. The community is lucky to have you living in its midst.'

32

The phone often rang at an inconvenient time. On this particular evening, Anna was about to get into the bath. She poised, wondering whether to ignore it. Somebody needing help? Libby? She couldn't leave it. She turned the taps off and grabbed a towel.

'Hello?'

'Anna?' A man's voice she didn't recognise.

'Yes, it is.'

'Greg McKenzie, Anna. How are you?'

'Oh hello, Greg! How nice to hear from you. I'm fine, thank you. How are you?'

'OK. Have the floodwaters receded while I've been away?'

'They have, thank goodness. It's going to take some time before everyone's back in their homes, but we're getting there.'

'That's good. I meant to check in, but I got called away suddenly. I had to go out to Dubai overnight to sort out a problem they were having there.'

'With a power station?'

'Yes, that's right. I've just got back. I wouldn't want you to think I'd forgotten about you, Anna.'

She laughed. 'The woman in the water?'

'Something like that. It was fun, wasn't it?'

'Yes, I suppose it was, really, once we knew everyone was safe. And it won't happen again for a hundred years, we're told.'

'Oh, I don't know about that! That's one area where we engineers are on shaky ground. It could happen again next week.'

'Don't say that, Greg!' she groaned. 'I've got to go to work.'

He laughed. 'Look, I was wondering if you're free next Saturday? If you are, do you fancy coming down here for the day? Remember, we did talk about the possibility?'

'I remember. That would be lovely, Greg.'

★ ★ ★

She caught a bus to Morpeth, and another one from there that took her into Newcastle. All the way, she tingled with excitement. This was a lovely day out for her, the kind she didn't have very often. Big city, here she came!

And there was Greg. At least, she hoped, there would be. She had a date! It was a long time since that had happened. She wondered which version of Greg she was going to meet — the difficult, miserable one she used to know; or the pleasant, helpful one she had come to know during the time of the floods. She thought she knew, actually. The man she had spoken to on the phone had been the new Greg.

She smiled as she wondered what

Greg's grandfather, old Willie McKenzie, would think about this. He would think she was pulling his leg if she ever told him. So she wouldn't. It was none of his business, anyway. This was about her and Greg. No-one else came into it.

* * *

Greg met her at the bus station. As the bus pulled in, she caught sight of him and waved. He spotted her and waved back, smiling. So that was settled, she thought with satisfaction. He was in a good mood. So was she!

'Good trip?' Greg asked, taking her hand.

'Excellent!' she assured him, kissing him on the cheek. 'The bus was right on time, too.'

'That's a wonder. Anyway, it's good to see you again.'

She smiled. 'Recovered from the soaking we gave you in Carlton?'

He chuckled. 'It took a while to dry the car out, as well as my clothes and shoes, but yes. Everything's fine here. What about there?'

She grimaced. 'We're getting there. A few people are not back in their own homes yet, as I said, including Miss Fenwick, but they will be soon, I hope. Otherwise, the clearing-up continues.'

'Seen anything of my grandad?'

'A bit. Not a lot. He's one of the lucky ones, thanks to you. He was able to return to his home early.'

'That might stop him complaining for a while,' Greg said with satisfaction.

'No, no! Be fair. He's not complained about anything at all. He's in fine fettle.'

'Oh? That's good. Right. Now where do you want to go first?'

'I was thinking about that. Do you know, I would just like to wander around a bit, and get used to being here. All these people — and all the shops! I don't come here very often. So it's like a foreign holiday for me.'

'Come on, then,' Greg said, chuckling. 'That's what we'll do.'

So they walked down Northumberland Street, past all the big shop windows and through the crowds. A young lad was busking, playing jaunty tunes on his fiddle. A man who might have been Eastern European smiled continuously as he played his accordion, and ducked his head to acknowledge the contributions passers-by left in a little cardboard box at his feet.

'Terrible so-called music!' Greg growled, wincing at the sound of the accordion.

'Dance music, isn't it?' Anna said. 'For a polka? Something like that.'

'Terrible, anyway. Ah! This is better.'

They stopped for a few minutes to listen to four men who might have been from somewhere in South America, as they belted out big tunes on trumpet and trombone, and a couple of brass instruments Anna didn't recognise.

'Better than a Sally Army band,' Greg said with enthusiasm.

Anna chuckled. 'Plenty of noise, anyway!'

'Too true! They're good, though. Fancy a coffee?'

She nodded happily and squeezed his hand.

33

After coffee in Fenwick's, the famous Newcastle department store, they drifted south to the Quayside, and the Tyne and all its wonderful bridges.

'How many are there?' Anna asked as they leant on the railings beside the river.

'At last count, I thought there were seven you could see from here,' Greg said, 'plus Scotswood Bridge, a couple of miles away but still in the city. Mind you, they could have built another one while I've been away.'

Anna laughed and put her arm through his. 'In our village, we only have the one,' she said, 'and that's just something they put up six or seven hundred years ago.'

'Bridges were bridges in those days,' Greg told her solemnly. 'None of this concrete and steel rubbish, like they use now. Your bridge will still be there when all these have disintegrated.'

'That's good to know,' she said, chuckling.

'Now, where next, do you think?'

Anna gazed across the river. 'How about the Baltic? I've never been there, but I've heard about it.' She had her eye on an old flour mill that had been saved from demolition and converted into a museum of contemporary art.

'Hm,' Greg said doubtfully. 'Still, if you've never been, maybe we should go so you can see what all the fuss is about.'

'You don't sound very approving?'

'No, no! Don't let me put you off. Anyway, it's a good place to have lunch.'

Once there, they took the lift to the sixth floor, where there was a classy restaurant, and then began to work their way back down the building, floor by floor, looking at the exhibitions on offer.

'Hm,' Anna said by the time they had reached the third floor. 'I see what you mean. Don't they have any paintings or sculptures?'

'Sorry,' Greg said. 'Only contemporary art here. Collections of junk, things that have been found, and splashes of paint intended to reveal what a demented mind looks like on the inside — that sort of thing.'

'I much prefer Libby Fenwick's paintings,' Anna said decisively. 'I've had enough of this lot. Let's get some lunch. There's somewhere here, you said. I hope you weren't thinking of that very expensive-looking restaurant at the top of the building?'

Greg laughed and shook his head. 'There's a decent café on the ground floor. We'll go there.'

* * *

In the afternoon Greg took her to his apartment overlooking the river. As he had said, it was indeed very modern.

234

'Wow!' Anna said, impressed as soon as they walked inside.

'You like?'

'I'll say!'

It was a tasteful confection of glass, stainless steel, hardwood floors, and expensive-looking rugs, some of them hanging on the walls.

'Did you do the interior design, Greg?'

He shook his head.

'Did you hire somebody?'

'No. She did it. That was her thing.'

Oh, dear! Anna thought. I've dropped a clanger. Presumably he was talking about his ex-wife.

'It's very nice.'

Greg glanced around as if evaluating things. Then he shrugged. 'It's all right, I suppose. I'm used to it.'

The apartment was rather like what you saw in glossy magazines, Anna thought. It wouldn't do in Carlton, but it was perfect for here. Downtown style? Something like that.

'The best thing about the apartment,

in my opinion,' Greg offered, 'is the view. Come and see.'

From the balcony window they could see just about the whole of the Quayside, the river and more bridges than she could count.

'Oh, yes,' Anna said quietly. 'I see what you mean. It's a wonderful view. I can see why you like living here.'

Greg smiled and took her hand. When he turned to look at her, she knew he was going to kiss her. And he did.

They clung together for some time, and Anna felt quite light-hearted by the time they parted and came up for air. Greg studied her with a smile, head on one side. She grinned and kissed the end of his nose before she stepped back.

'That will do for now!' she said, laughing happily.

'A glass of wine?' he asked.

She nodded. 'Thank you. Then you can tell me what you've been doing all these weeks since I last saw you.'

He told her about his work and his travels. She found herself thinking what a glamorous life he led. First-class air travel, five-star hotels, expensive restaurants, interesting places. It was a far cry from the life she knew. It sounded absolutely wonderful.

When she said so, Greg said, 'You think? Well, my ex-wife didn't agree. She tried coming with me, and she tried stopping at home. Neither way suited her. She appreciated the money I made, all right,' he added, waving a hand around at the apartment, 'but nothing else about how we lived.'

'It's hard for me to believe,' Anna said, shaking her head. 'I would love the chance to visit those places. Not the fancy hotels and restaurants so much, perhaps, but seeing different countries and cultures.'

'They're not like here, you know.'

She laughed. 'No, I don't suppose they are.'

'They're all either too hot or too cold, too expensive or too poor. People don't speak the language. They wear funny clothes.'

'Oh, stop it, Greg!' she said, laughing. 'I'm sure your wife wasn't that ignorant.'

'No, perhaps not,' he admitted.

'She was very lucky to have the chance to see such places.'

Greg nodded. 'That was what I thought. In the years when I worked on Tyneside, I would have thought myself lucky to get the chance, too.'

Something was on his mind, she realised as he dried up. What was he thinking? About his ex-wife? The wasted opportunities?

'I'm going to Qatar for six months the week after next,' he said suddenly. 'Want to come with me?'

She stared at him, wondering if he was teasing her. Surely it wasn't a serious question? But, as the seconds ticked away, she realised he was.

'Me?'

Greg nodded. 'Why not? You might like it.'

'I'm sure I would.'

'We get on well together — after a rocky start! Maybe we should hold on to that, and see what happens?'

She smiled, a little nervously. 'I like the idea, but six months? There's my job to consider, as well as other things. Let me think about it.'

'Sure.' He grinned, and added, 'After a taste of the high life, you might not want to go to work any more — never mind back to your old job!'

34

There was a lot to think about over the remainder of the weekend, and on Sunday night Anna didn't get much sleep. She wasn't in any doubt about what lay behind Greg's invitation. It wasn't simply an offer to see a bit of the world for free. He was a lonely man, embittered by the departure of a wife who for some reason had tired of life with him, and he wanted — not to put too fine a point on it — a replacement. He wanted company, someone with whom he could share his life. There was nothing wrong with that. In the end, she thought, it's what most of us want.

Well, then? Why hesitate? There wasn't a better offer on the table. I'm not hesitating, she told herself. Not really. Not actually . . . hesitating, as such. I just need to think things through, and make sure I get it right. It would be a big leap for me, and I have a lot to lose if it doesn't work out.

Oh, yeah? A lot to lose? Like what?

Well, I have a house and a job. I am part of a community that I like. I live in a place I love.

And? What else?

That's a lot in itself! she thought defiantly. It's a lot to put at risk.

On the other side, of course, she didn't necessarily want to spend her life alone, and she did like Greg. Now, at least, she did. It had been different when she first knew him, but now she could see the real person behind that tough exterior. And they seemed to get on well together.

They were attracted to each other physically, too. Not, perhaps, earth-shatteringly, madly, wildly so, but there had been electricity passing between them when they kissed, and neither of them was a teenager any more anyway.

Greg was an interesting man, too, and he had a lot going for him. She also knew that financially she would be secure for life if she joined forces with Greg, regardless of whether or not she had a job. That was something else to bear in mind. It wouldn't be a life lived in poverty.

That apartment! she thought then with a smile. She had never been in anything like it. Stunning was the word to describe it. Greg had seemed keen to have someone refurbish it. So she wouldn't be stuck with his ex-wife's design preferences. But where to start? She doubted she could do any better with it.

Finally, she came to the elephant in the room. Greg was Greg. He wasn't David Wilson. She shrugged. For all the interest David had ever shown in her, she might as well forget him and move on. She was old enough, and realistic enough, to know that.

So then?

She had promised to let Greg know her answer in a couple of days, and that was what she would do.

* * *

Her mood wasn't great on Monday morning, not after most of a night spent agonising over what to do about Greg's invitation. It wasn't made easier by her section head calling an early meeting.

'Do we have to do this now, Arthur?' asked Eunice plaintively. 'I'm really busy.'

'Yes, we do. It's important.' Arthur settled his glasses firmly on his nose, peered round at the four of them, and added, 'Anybody else got any complaints?'

Anna simply smiled and shook her head. It was the best she could manage.

Pete said he would like to know if there would be a pay rise this year, at last. The union were saying there wouldn't be, which was outrageous. Arthur smiled patiently at him, and said he had no idea.

'What do you want to talk about, Arthur?' asked Francine, the other member of the team.

Arthur leant back in his chair, cleared his throat and said, 'This won't take long. I think you all know the next budget settlement is going to be difficult. There's no secret about that.'

'What else is new?' Pete grumbled. 'We hear that every year.'

'What's new,' Arthur said testily, 'is that this time it affects us directly. I thought I should tell you that one of our jobs will have to go. In other words, there will be three of you in the section, not four.'

To stop the clamour that immediately started, Arthur held up his hand and said, 'There's some way to go yet before it's final, but I'm told on very good authority that it is going to happen. I very much regret that, but we have to get used to the idea, I'm afraid.

'My hope is that it may suit one of you to volunteer for redundancy. The terms would be quite generous, I believe. Failing that . . . ' Arthur shrugged and added, 'At this moment

244

in time, I have no idea at present which one of you will lose his or her job.'

'Well, it's not going to be me!' Pete said furiously. 'I've got a mortgage and two young kids to pay for, as well as a wife.'

'Quite,' Arthur said with a sigh.

'My elderly mother lives with me,' Eunice said angrily. 'There's no way I can afford to lose my job.'

'Nor me,' Francine said calmly. 'Not with my responsibilities. I can tell you now, Arthur, it's not going to happen — not without a fight that will give the council a very black name. I shall go to an industrial tribunal and every court in the land, claiming wrongful dismissal, sexual discrimination, and anything else I can think of. I shall go to Brussels, and the European Court of Human Rights!'

Then they all looked at Anna, who found she had nothing to say. Her morning had started poorly anyway. Now she just felt empty, drained and unable to think straight. It felt as if somebody had pulled the plug on her life.

'Excuse me,' she said, getting to her feet. 'I don't feel well.'

Arthur nodded and stood up himself. 'I don't suppose any of us feels well,' he said quietly. 'Let's all get back to work. But I want all of you to give it some thought. We'll have to return to the issue later. It won't go away.'

* * *

By the end of the day, on the bus on the way home, Anna knew what she was going to do. Arthur's announcement had tipped the scales for her. She knew she would have to be the one who lost her job. All the others had dependants. She didn't. If she held on to her job, and one of the others lost theirs, she wouldn't be able to look her colleagues in the eye, or forgive herself either.

Her situation was now far less complicated than it had seemed over the weekend. Now she had far less to lose. She would accept Greg's invitation, and travel hopefully.

35

Just after she got in from work, Anna took a phone call from Mrs Henderson at *Dunroamin*.

'I'm sorry to bother you, Anna, but Libby isn't very well,' Mrs Henderson said. 'Nothing serious — don't worry! I think it's just the virus that's been going around the village.'

'Headache, sore throat, stuffed-up nose? Feeling tired all the time?'

'Yes, that's it. Do you know it?'

'I've had it!'

Mrs Henderson laughed. 'Poor you! But perhaps I shouldn't be bothering you?'

'No, no! What is it? How can I help?'

'Well ... You know Libby, don't you?'

'Indeed I do.'

'Then you won't be surprised to hear that she's a bit grumpy at the moment.

I have the impression she's tired of me. In fact, she's rather rude at times — telling me this afternoon what to do with the soft-boiled egg I'd brought her for her tea!'

Anna chuckled. 'That sounds like Libby! She can be very impatient, and she does get frustrated. I can imagine her not taking very kindly to feeling under the weather. Don't worry, Mrs Henderson.'

'I'm not worried, exactly. I feel sorry for her. I just wondered if you could come over for half an hour to see her? You get on with her very well, I know, and I just thought she might appreciate seeing your friendly face for a change.'

Anna laughed. 'I'll come over. No problem. Just give me half an hour to get changed and have a bite to eat. I've not long been in from work.'

'Oh, just get changed and come over! I'll make something for your tea. Would scrambled eggs or an omelette do?'

'That would be wonderful!'

'You can have it with Libby. Perhaps

she'll eat something, if you're here with her.'

* * *

'I don't mind you coming to see me from time to time,' Libby confided. 'You're a sensible woman. I can talk to you. But some of these others . . . Oh, I know they mean well! They are very kind, and so on, and I am grateful to be able to stay here. All the same . . . '

'It's not the same as being in your own home?'

'That's it, exactly! How long do you think it will be before I can go back?'

'Just a few more days. David says that if you identify the appliances you want in those catalogues I gave you, he'll soon have them brought and fitted.'

'That's very good of him — and you, too. I don't know how I'd have managed without you both.'

'You'd have managed, Libby. I know you would.'

Libby seemed to drift off for a few

250

moments. She really wasn't well, Anna thought with a grimace. This wasn't like her. It was the virus. Everyone that had it complained about feeling worn out for a week or two.

'She might have helped, I suppose,' Libby murmured softly, her eyes closed.

'Pardon?'

'My daughter. She might have helped. I don't know, though. Probably she hates me. That's what happens, isn't it?'

Anna was taken aback, electrified. Did she really hear Libby saying all that?

She leant forward and said gently, 'Your daughter? I didn't know you had a daughter, Libby?'

'Oh, yes. A long time ago.'

Was she rambling in her sleep? Dreaming? Or was she referring to the baby she had once had?

'The baby was a girl?'

'Yes. A dear little thing. I couldn't be bothered with her, of course. Not at my age.'

Her age? Anna wondered if she meant now or then. Was she too old now, or had she been too young then?

'Anyway, they insisted I was too young. It's a pity, really.'

'You were very young, I suppose,' Anna said softly.

Libby nodded, opened her eyes and struggled to sit up. 'Just a girl,' she said with a sad smile. Then she looked horrified. 'What did I just say?' she demanded quickly. 'Was I talking rubbish? I do that sometimes, you know.'

Anna shook her head firmly. 'Not rubbish, Libby. No, of course not.' She took a deep breath and ploughed on. 'You were talking about your daughter.'

'Daughter? What daughter?' Libby gave a forced laugh. 'You're mistaken, dear. I have no daughter. I must have been dreaming.'

Anna shook her head. 'I don't think so, Libby. It's all right if you don't want to talk about it. I don't mind. But I knew you'd had a baby when you were very young. I just didn't know it was a girl.'

After a long silence, Libby said slowly, 'No-one knew. It was kept very quiet. My parents saw to that.'

'Perhaps it was a good thing?'

'Perhaps. At the time . . . A young girl having a baby out of wedlock was a terrible thing in those days, you know?'

Anna nodded. 'I understand.'

'I was too young to look after a baby anyway. I was still at school, for heaven's sake! My parents were right, and very sensible about it. The family did well, I suppose, the way they handled it.'

'You went away, didn't you?'

'Yes. They sent me, and the child, to live with Great Aunt Ada in Edgbaston, in Birmingham. There were lots of servants there, and nannies and such-like too.'

'The baby wasn't sent to an orphanage? That often happened, didn't it, in those days?'

'Oh, no! Father wouldn't have that.

Nor would Mother. I was happy enough with the arrangement.'

'What about Willie, though?'

'Willie?' Libby asked with a frown. 'Who's that?'

'Willie McKenzie.'

'I don't understand. What's he got to do with it?'

'Well,' Anna said uncertainly, 'the father does have some rights, surely?'

Libby stared at her with amazement. 'Is that what you think?'

'Well . . . '

Libby started to chuckle. Then she laughed and shook her head. 'Willie McKenzie! What's he been telling you?'

'Nothing, really,' Anna said, stung. She gestured helplessly. 'He was in love with you, wasn't he? I just assumed . . . '

'Oh, yes! Willie was in love with me, all right,' Libby admitted carelessly. 'But they all were in those days, all the boys. Willie was a nice boy, too. But he was romantic, and rather silly. I couldn't bear it. I couldn't be bothered with someone like that!'

Libby stopped talking and began to laugh again. 'Willie McKenzie, indeed!'

36

'What about you, Anna? How have you been?'

Anna was surprised, astonished almost, to hear Libby asking such a question. It seemed so out of character, she thought with an inward smile.

'Oh, I've been busy, as usual. Full of busy. But until today everything seemed fine,' she said with a grimace. 'Well, that's not quite right. Even after today, everything will be OK, I think. Like they say, as one door slams shut, another one opens. I'll be all right.'

Libby stared at her. 'This isn't like you, Anna. What on earth happened today?'

Anna shrugged and said, 'It's a long story, Libby. You don't want to hear it.'

'No, no! That's not true. I do want to hear it. What happened?'

'I lost my job. I'm to be made

redundant because the council needs to make cost savings.'

'And you're a cost saving?'

Anna nodded. 'A voluntary redundancy, they call it. One of the four jobs in my section has to go, and the other three people all have dependants. So it had to be me that volunteered.'

Still staring at her, Libby said, 'Don't tell me you volunteered?'

'Well . . . ' Anna said helplessly, wishing now that she had kept quiet.

'Isn't that just like you? You never think of yourself, do you?'

Anna glanced at her watch. 'I must be going soon, Libby.'

Libby shook her head, as if she couldn't believe how stupid Anna had been.

'But things will work out, I think, Libby. Don't worry about me. Gregory McKenzie, Willie's grandson, has invited me to go with him for six months to somewhere in the Middle East. He does a lot of work there.'

'Really?'

It was very clear what Libby thought of that, as well. She didn't even have to say anything. In fact, she didn't say much at all after that. She just said she wanted to study the catalogues Anna had brought, and she would decide what fridge and cooker she wanted.

'And a washing machine,' Anna pointed out. 'Don't forget you need a replacement for that, as well. And a freezer.'

'I know, I know! Just leave me with it. I'll sort it out.'

Seeing Libby brimming with a restored sense of purpose, Anna made her escape. She had plenty to do herself that evening. She wanted a good long soak in a hot bath, too. That was the best way she knew of healing damage and sorting out what to do next.

Mrs Henderson caught her on the way out. 'I heard Libby laughing, Anna, and I've not heard that sound for a day or two. I'm so glad you were able to come. Your visit has done her the world of good. Me too, actually!'

Anna smiled ruefully. 'Without meaning to, I told Libby something she thought was absolutely absurd. That's why she was laughing.'

'Well, try to think of something absurd for me to tell her!' Mrs Henderson said with a chuckle. 'I don't like to see Libby with a long face.'

Somehow, Anna didn't feel like going straight home when she got outside. She decided to visit Liza Tully instead. She hadn't seen her for a few days. There might be another prescription for her to collect, and perhaps some more shopping to be done.

It flashed through her mind to wonder what would happen when she went away with Greg. Could she find someone else to do these things for Liza? The family didn't seem very keen, but perhaps they could be prevailed upon. She would ask David if he could talk to them.

David, she thought with a wince. That was someone else she needed to tell. She wasn't looking forward to that either.

Fortunately, Liza was in good form. Happy as she was to be back home again, Anna had the impression she was still excited about everything that had happened during the floods. Admittedly, her house had not been totally inundated, but there had been damage and she had been evacuated. Still, she seemed to have enjoyed the experience. It had been a change, as she was so fond of saying whenever anything out of the ordinary occurred.

'And now you've had the decorators in?' Anna said, glancing around the living room. 'What a good job they've done, too.'

'Do you like it, the wallpaper?' Liza asked shyly. 'I chose it myself.'

'It's lovely, Liza.'

Dear God, she thought. How can she bear to be surrounded by these floral patterns all day long? The new wallpaper was like something from the nineteenth century. She shuddered to think what Greg McKenzie, or — even more — his ex-wife would think. Still, she thought with amusement, Liza was almost from that time herself. Why shouldn't she surround herself with the things she admired when she was young?

'The insurance will pay for it,' Liza said with satisfaction.

Even more reason to be happy!

'And your grandson did the work, I understand?'

'Jason, yes. He works for himself, you know? He has his own little business.'

'Good for him. And there's another grandson, one with a plumbing business, isn't there?'

'My great-nephew, Michael. That's Alice and Freddie's boy. He's another who's doing very well for himself.'

Anna nodded. 'You're lucky, Liza, to have such a talented and industrious family, especially at a time like this. They've looked after you, haven't they?'

'Oh, they have! They've been wonderful. I don't know what I would have done without them.'

'You'd have struggled along, just as Fred Baker is doing. Poor Fred! We're helping him as much as we can, from the church, but it's going to be a while before he's settled back in his house again. As we said before, it's a problem when you don't have a family to support you.'

Liza nodded. 'I feel sorry for Fred. It's been difficult for him since his wife died.'

Anna nodded.

'He shouldn't have been, you know. On his own, I mean. But it was the times,' Liza said with a sigh. 'And his poor wife couldn't have children herself, more's the pity.'

'How could Fred not have been on his own, Liza? I don't understand. What do you mean?'

'Oh, nothing! Me and my big mouth. That's all it was.'

Anna waited, but nothing more seemed to be forthcoming. She changed the subject. 'David Wilson and I think we can get Libby Fenwick back into her house very soon. In a few days, perhaps. Things are not finished, but she can be back in the house while the work continues. She's looking forward to that.'

'I'm sure she is. I know how she will feel.' Liza was lost in thought for a moment. Then she said, 'Do you think Libby's changed at all?'

'In what way?'

Liza shrugged. 'When I saw her in the church hall she seemed a bit different to how I remembered her.'

Anna smiled. 'A lot of things had changed since you'd last seen her, Liza. Besides, everybody was different during the floods.'

'I suppose so. Yes, I expect you're right.'

Another few moments, while Anna prepared to depart, and then Liza said suddenly, 'She was unlucky, as well, you know.'

'Who?'

'Libby Fenwick.'

'Oh, I don't know about that. She's had a wonderful career, and seen a bit of the world. She's a well-known artist, you know?'

Liza made a dismissive gesture. 'That doesn't mean a thing, in the end. Where's her family? Where's the love?'

Anna nodded and sighed. 'I know what you mean, Liza. You were right about her having a baby, by the way. Libby told me herself.'

'Yes,' Liza said slowly, 'and she wasn't allowed to keep it, was she? And now she's on her own, with no family. Like I said, she's been unlucky, really, the same as Fred Baker has.'

That was probably about right, Anna thought. But hold on! Was it all down to luck? Surely not?

As if reading her mind, Liza said, 'And how are you doing, pet? Did you take my advice?'

Puzzled, Anna said, 'What advice was that, Liza?'

'Don't wait for luck. And don't wait for a shy man to say the right thing either. Go on and ask him!'

'What on earth are you talking about, Liza?'

'That David Wilson, of course! You'll wait for ever if you wait for him to get round to it.'

'Liza Tully!' Anna cried in consternation. 'Don't you dare say anything else. I'm going!'

37

Her lack of mobility really got to Anna at times. She could get to work all right, by bus and by arranging lifts, but going anywhere outside the village spontaneously was out of the question. Emergency trips could also be a problem, and she seemed to have to undertake more and more of those to distant hospitals as friends and neighbours got older. So when her widowed elderly next-door neighbour, Mary Pattinson, announced that she was giving up her car, it got her thinking.

'I never was a good driver,' Mary said wistfully. 'And now, what with my arthritis and my eyesight, it's more difficult than ever. Then there's the cost — insurance, tax, repairs, petrol, and everything. I only go around the village anyway. So it's not worth keeping a car. It will be more sensible for me to get a taxi for the trips I want to make.'

As Mary was well into her eighties and not in good health, Anna found it hard to disagree with her.

'It's a lovely little car, though, isn't it? What a shame. Will you sell it?'

'The man in the garage said he'll take it off my hands. It's in good condition, but it's ten years old. So it's not worth anything. A couple of hundred pounds, the man said. It is a shame, you're right, but that's all it's worth.'

Anna thought quickly. The car was a little Renault that she knew was in good condition. Unlike David's car, it seemed to start easily, whatever the weather.

'Would you consider selling it to me, Mary? Whatever the man in the garage offers you for it, I'll match it.'

Why not? She had the money. And she was tired of begging lifts and having to work out how to get from one place to another. The car could sit in her empty garage while she was away with Greg, and if things didn't work out with him it would still be here waiting for her.

'You, dear?' Mary looked at her doubtfully. 'You don't drive, do you?'

'I can drive. I do have a licence. I've had one for many years. I just don't have a car!'

'Well, let me go inside and fetch the keys,' Mary said. 'You drive it around a bit, and then tell me if you want it.'

A day or two later, Anna had a car that was registered, taxed and insured in her own name. She took it out for her first long run, and more by chance than design found herself heading for Nether Edge. Then, driving into the village, she saw David's mother. It looked as if she was walking home from the village shop. Anna stopped, opened the window and called to her.

'Would you like a lift, Mrs Wilson?'

Mrs Wilson peered uncertainly for a moment. Then she smiled. 'Oh, hello, Anna! What are you doing here?'

'Test driving my new car. I've just bought it from a neighbour. Like it?'

'It looks very nice.'

'Well, it's old, but it goes fine. Better than David's anyway. Jump in. I'll run you home.'

'That's kind of you. This shopping is heavy. You must come in for a cup of tea with me.'

Anna had found Mrs Wilson very easy to talk to on her first visit, and this time it was no different. She was a charming woman, and seemed pleased to see Anna again.

'I don't get many visitors,' she said. 'So it's lovely to have you here. Isn't it a working day for you, though?'

'It is, or it should be, but I've taken the day off to sort out about the car. Insurance and so on.'

Mrs Wilson poured the tea. 'It's a lovely little car. Having it should make your life a lot easier. I know I would be lost without mine. I don't go very far in it, but I can't walk everywhere I do want to go.'

'I know what you mean. I'm the same. Living out here, you really do need a car. Life can be difficult without one. Funnily enough, though, I've got the car just as my life is about to change anyway. I won't need it in Newcastle. You can travel everywhere around Tyneside by Metro.'

'Oh? I didn't know that. You're moving into the city?'

'It looks like it. I'm being made redundant from my job, and I've met someone nice who lives in Newcastle.'

Mrs Wilson was quiet for a moment. Then she said, 'I'm sorry about your job, Anna, and to hear that you're leaving. I know David will be too.'

'David? Oh, he'll find plenty of others in the church to help him.'

'I wasn't thinking of that. I meant he'll miss you in a personal sense.'

Anna smiled ruefully. 'Oh, I don't think so. Not really. Anyway, I'll be coming backwards and forwards after I get back from the trip we're going to make to the Middle East. I'll still have the cottage in Carlton, after all.'

'Yes?' Mrs Wilson smiled brightly.

'Well, you must do what is best for you, Anna. But I know you will be missed. Lots of people will be disappointed to hear you're leaving, David most of all.'

Anna chuckled. 'David and I will still be friends, Mrs Wilson! Just like we always have been. We've known each other all our lives.'

'Yes, of course.'

Anna wished now that she hadn't said anything about her plans. Mrs Wilson seemed so disappointed about them. In an effort to cheer her up, she changed the subject.

'David tells me you like to paint — that you're quite an artist, in fact?'

Mrs Wilson laughed. 'I don't think you could call me an artist! It's true, though. I do like to paint. I always have. In fact, I enjoy painting and drawing almost as much as I enjoy gardening. It comes from my mother, I suppose. It's in the genes.'

'Oh?'

'Not that I ever really knew my mother. She disappeared from my life very early on, and I was brought up by relatives. But Mother went to art school and became a very good artist, I'm led to believe. She had a fine career, too.'

Anna smiled. 'What a strange but interesting life you seem to have led.'

'Oh, it's true!' Mrs Wilson laughed 'But a happy one. I certainly can't complain.'

Anna wondered if she really believed that, and decided that she probably did. After all, she seemed contented enough, and she had brought up a son to be proud of. Not a conventional life, perhaps, but was there such a thing these days anyway?

'Where do you do your painting?' Anna asked, glancing round.

'Oh, not in here! It would be far too messy. I use a spare bedroom, and keep everything in the one place. Would you like to see what I do?'

'Oh, yes please! I would love to. I must warn you, though. I shall be wildly jealous. I really admire creative people.'

'You needn't be jealous of me, Anna. Given the time and the interest, anyone could do what I do. I'm not creative at all.'

Mrs Wilson's modest denial was soon seen to be misleading. There was very little wallpaper to be seen on the walls of the spare bedroom. Every square inch seemed to be covered with her paintings.

'Goodness!' Anna said with astonishment. 'You need a bigger house. I've never seen so many pictures.'

'Well,' Mrs Wilson said judiciously, 'I don't think a bigger house would be sensible, but I have wondered if I really do need a bedroom. A second room to hang my collection in would be ideal. Either that, or stop painting!'

Anna laughed. 'Oh, no! Don't ever think of doing that. Painting is a lovely hobby, and you're obviously very good at it.'

'Well . . . I do my best.'

'A very good best,' Anna said firmly. 'Do you sell your paintings?'

273

'A few. I exhibit here and there, in local galleries, and occasionally someone buys one.'

'I'm not surprised. A painting is far better than a photograph, especially as a memento of a holiday, or as a gift.'

The paintings were nearly all watercolours of local landscapes. Mrs Wilson clearly made good use of what was on offer within a short distance of her home. The hills and the moors, the rivers and the patches of woodland, all looked pleasingly familiar to Anna's eye. Having said that, she also knew they were the kind of paintings that could be seen wherever an art class or amateur painters exhibited their work.

Lovely, delicate watercolours of familiar scenes, but not surprisingly she didn't think Mrs Wilson was a top-class, innovative artist. What she seemed to be was someone who simply enjoyed painting as a hobby. In that, she was very fortunate.

Then Anna saw a blaze of colour — reds, blues and yellows — and stopped before a painting that stood out every bit as much as the proverbial sore thumb. She stopped dead and stared at the canvas.

'My goodness, Mrs Wilson!'

'Lydia, please. Mrs Wilson sounds terribly formal.'

'Lydia,' Anna said absently.

'Do you like this picture?'

Anna nodded. She was gripped by it, her mind working feverishly to process what she was looking at.

'It's my mother's — the only one of hers that I have.'

Anna reeled, in her excitement almost falling over. 'Really?'

'My grandparents gave it me. She had given it to them, and they cherished it, but I don't think they ever really liked it. Probably far too modern for them.'

Anna longed to sit down and think. This was absolutely extraordinary, and totally unexpected. She scarcely dared even to try to think it through, and she knew she couldn't possibly say anything until she had. The last thing she wanted to do was to upset anybody.

'I've always assumed,' Lydia continued, 'that she painted this either during or after a holiday somewhere on the Mediterranean coast, possibly Provence. But it may have been Greece. The colours, you see? They're so different to what we know here.'

Anna just nodded.

'At any rate, I've always liked it, and wanted it with me,' Lydia said with a wan smile. 'It's all I have of hers.'

That sounded so unbearably sad that, unable to help herself, Anna reached out and hugged her. It seemed to be the least she could do.

38

Anna had a lot to think about, and some connections to make. She had never lost the sense that someone had emptied a box of jigsaw pieces onto her desk. Thanks to Lydia, she believed she could see now how the picture all came together. Before she had spoken to Lydia again, everything had just seemed a jumble of unconnected and random facts and circumstances, people and relationships.

So what did she know?

Well, to start at the beginning, Miss Libby Fenwick grew up with her parents in Sunnyside House, in the village of Carlton. She had a lovely early life. She was clever and vivacious, and very charismatic. Chased after by various boys as a teenager — although the term wouldn't have been used then, of course — she succumbed to the charms of one of them, and became pregnant at too young an age.

To contain the scandal, for such it was in those days, she was sent to live with a branch of the family in Birmingham. A great-aunt — obviously well-to-do — effectively brought up the baby, and steered Libby through her teens and into womanhood.

Libby went to some private school in London, and then on to art college. She developed into a talented artist, and launched into a successful career as a painter. Meanwhile, her daughter had been effectively abandoned, to be raised by her great-aunt, assisted by her parents. The child, Lydia, stayed often with her grandparents during school holidays, and came to know the area around Carlton well.

Eventually, Lydia embarked on an adult life herself. She married, and had a child of her own, a boy she and her husband called David. When her husband died at a young age, Lydia came back north to the area where she had spent happy times as a child. By then her grandparents were gone. But she settled in a nearby village, where she raised her son and enjoyed a quiet life. She had inherited her mother's interest in painting, but not perhaps her talent. For her, art was a satisfying hobby.

Much more recently, Libby herself returned to the area, and to the house bequeathed to her by her grandmother. She led a reclusive life there, for reasons unknown, and seemed to have forgotten the child she had brought into the world. At least, she had no idea where the child was, or what had become of her.

How extraordinary! Anna thought, shaking her head. The two women, mother and daughter, were back within touching distance again, if only they knew it. The question was: would they *want* to know it? Would they appreciate being told?

Anna put the question aside for the moment.

Now, what else was left to sort out? she wondered.

Well, one question was: who was Lydia's father? It didn't seem to be Willie McKenzie, who for a time she had assumed it to be. Well, then. Someone who had never been mentioned to her at all? Perhaps.

What else? David, of course. He was Libby's grandson, after all, even if neither of them knew it. Would they want to know it?

Oh, dear! What am I to do about all this? she asked herself, holding her head in her hands. Anything, or nothing?

There was something else she needed to sort out, and it took priority. David's mother had put it in her mind. She spent an afternoon walking by the river, which was now back to its normal restful self, all ambition to permanently occupy the village set aside.

The river might have been back to gentle, soothing normality, but Anna struggled to find tranquillity along its bank. Far too much was going on in her head. In the end, she gave up and went to see David, thinking that perhaps she should have done that a long time ago.

To her surprise, the door to the office in the builder's yard was closed. A 'Closed' sign was hanging on the window set in the door.

'He's not there,' a man stacking lengths of timber said with satisfaction.

'I can see that. Where is he? Do you know?'

The man shook his head. 'Something must have come up.'

Anna sighed and walked off, feeling frustrated. Nothing was easy, it seemed. Not even this.

★ ★ ★

Back at home, she procrastinated or prevaricated — she wasn't sure which it was! — but in the end she picked up the phone and made the call. She had to do it. Maybe she was being stupid, throwing such an opportunity away.

Perhaps she would regret it. Who could tell? But she had to do it.

'Hi, Anna! How are you doing?'

'Hello, Greg. All right, I suppose. I've lost my job, but that doesn't really matter. Greg, I have to tell you that I'm sorry, very sorry, but I can't go with you. My life is here. Living as you do wouldn't suit me. I would become unhappy, and then so would you. I'm just not the person you need, I'm afraid.'

After a pause, Greg said, 'You're sure about this, are you?'

'I am. I am now. I appreciate what you offered me, but I can't do it. I just hope you do find someone soon to share your life. I really do. That's all I have to say, Greg. And I really am sorry.'

'It's a pity,' he said, but that was all he said. He seemed to accept there was no point discussing it further.

Afterwards, she felt relief. It was over, her brief flirtation with the idea of the high life. She had always known, really, that it wasn't for her. Perhaps Greg had, too. So that was that.

39

Now who could this be? she wondered glancing at the kitchen clock. What a time to come! Just as I'm preparing tea.

'David!' she said anxiously when she opened the door. 'What's wrong? What's happened?'

He shrugged and gave her a tired smile. 'May I come in for a moment?'

'Yes, of course.'

She stood aside and let him in, and then smiled and directed him into the living room. 'I was forgetting. You haven't been here before, have you?'

He shook his head. Then he stood awkwardly and glanced around. 'It's very nice. I admire your taste in furnishings.'

She laughed. 'My grandmother's taste, you mean. I've altered very little since I moved in. I haven't had the money or the time, to be honest. But I liked it as it was anyway. Gran was a very homely person, like me. What can I do for you, David? Would you like coffee?'

He shook his head.

'Please sit down. You're making the room seem small!'

'I'd rather not, if you don't mind. You might soon be asking me to leave.'

She stared at him, noting how discomfited he was. 'Why? What's happened, David?'

He swallowed awkwardly and made a start. 'I went to see Mother this afternoon. I don't know why, but I did.'

'Oh? I saw her earlier, as well,' Anna said, suddenly gripped by concern. 'She was all right then. Oh, David what's happened to her?'

'Nothing!' He shook his head. 'Don't worry about that. She's fine. But she gave me some disturbing news.'

He looked around again and waved vaguely, as if he didn't know what to say.

'David?'

'She said you're leaving, Anna — that you've found somebody else. You're moving into Newcastle.'

She stared at him in disbelief.

'I don't want you to go, Anna. Really. I don't think I could stand it if you did. There now! I've said it. God, I'm so embarrassed. I feel so inept.'

'No, you're not, David,' Anna said calmly, smiling with relief. 'You're none of those things. Of course you're not.

''Somebody else', is it?' she added with a coquettish smile. 'Somebody other than you, you mean?'

He sighed, and shrugged. 'I don't know what to say.'

'Come on, David! Sit down on the sofa with me.'

He sat down tentatively and looked at her with caution.

'I'm not going anywhere, David. Really. I changed my mind after talking to your mother. In fact, I called at your office this afternoon to tell you as much. But you weren't there.'

'I shut the place up early. I went to see Mother.'

'So you said.'

'You're not leaving?'

She shook her head. 'Definitely not. David, we've got to stop this endless circling around each other, and tell each other how we feel. That's another thing I intended saying to you this afternoon.

'It's gone on long enough — too long! We're neither of us getting any younger, as my mother would point out. I only considered taking up with somebody else because . . . '

'I love you, Anna,' David said gently. 'I always have. I just didn't know how to tell you.'

'Oh, David! And you're someone who can speak to anyone!'

He shrugged.

'How silly we've been,' she said softly. 'I just assumed you weren't interested in me. Anyway, this morning, after talking to your mother, I decided that if you were not going to say anything, then I would. I love you, too, David. There now! What do you think of that?'

'Give us a kiss!' he said, chuckling with apparent relief.

She did, and it felt wonderful.

Later, they tried to talk sensibly about the future, but it was difficult. They were both too absorbed by the moment. It was one they wanted to enjoy, and make last as long as possible.

'I'll help,' Anna promised. 'With everything.'

'I know.' David smiled. 'You already do.'

'We'll do things together, a real partnership. I'll support you, and I know you'll support me. Where will we live, though?'

'Well, I'm not particularly attached to my house. But let's just leave that for the moment,' he suggested. 'All right?'

She nodded. 'Actually, there are other things I want to talk to you about, David.'

And there were. Big and difficult things, though it was easier to speak of them now the biggest thing of all had been settled between them.

'Oh? What have you got in mind?'

She took a deep breath, and hoped she was doing the right thing.

'You have a grandmother, David, and she lives in Carlton.'

He nodded and smiled. 'Miss Fenwick.'

'You knew?' she said with astonishment.

'Yes.'

'Does your mother know, too?'

He nodded again. 'She knows. She told me.'

'And does Libby know about both of you?'

He shook his head. 'We felt we had to keep out of her way. So we've never approached her, or said anything to anybody.'

'Because?'

He shrugged.

'You didn't want to impose on her? Is that the reason? Too much history?'

'All of that.'

Anna thought quickly, and something else came to mind. 'But that's why you were so worried about her when the flooding began? You were keeping an eye on her from a distance?'

'Yes. That's right. I didn't want to favour her over other people, but I did want to make sure she was all right.'

'I suppose you couldn't have said anything to me?' Anna said reproachfully. 'No, of course not. You just couldn't.'

'I'm sorry. Mother didn't want . . .'

'I understand, David. Don't worry about it. I think I've got most of it sorted out now.'

They sat in silence, holding hands, for a few moments. Then David asked, 'What made you decide to speak to me about . . . about us?'

She chuckled. 'I'm every bit as bad as you when it comes to speaking of personal matters. It's so difficult. I hope you don't mind!'

'It was just something Liza Tully said. I think she must have known how we feel about each other. She said that you were shy, and that if I waited for you to say something, I would wait for ever! I decided she was right, and I'd better say something before it was too late.'

'I'm so very glad you did.'

'There's something else I want to ask you, David. Do you know who your grandfather is, or was?'

He shook his head. 'No idea. Mother doesn't know either.'

Anna nodded thoughtfully. She believed she could help answer that question, if they wanted her to.

40

Lydia clapped her hands with excitement when they told her. 'Will it be a long engagement?' she asked.

Anna shook her head. 'No. It won't.'

'We've known each other most of our lives,' David contributed. 'So there's no need for that.'

'I'm so pleased, and proud!' Lydia said, suspiciously close to tears. Then she gave Anna another hug and took herself off to the kitchen — more to collect herself than to put the kettle on, Anna suspected.

She looked at David, and smiled.

'That's someone else we've pleased,' he said softly.

She laughed.

★   ★   ★

Libby was in a strange mood when Anna visited her next. She was in better health, though, the virus defeated and energy levels restored. What was it that was a little unusual about her? Anna found it hard to put her finger on it, but something was different. Perhaps it would work its way to the surface if she was patient.

'I'm so pleased to see you, my dear,' Libby said with a welcoming smile. 'There's something I wanted to talk to you about. How is my house?'

Anna laughed. 'Straight to the point, eh, Libby? I don't blame you. Well, I'm happy to be able to tell you that we think you could move back in by the end of the week. It's Tuesday now . . . Friday, say?'

'Perfect. I shall look forward to it.'

'David and I will help you settle back in.'

'Thank you. You're very kind.'

It wasn't quite the fulsome response Anna had anticipated. Libby seemed to have something else on her mind.

'What?' Anna asked with a knowing smile.

'I beg your pardon?'

'What do you want to say? There's something else, isn't there?'

Libby laughed, seeming a little embarrassed. 'You know me so well!' she spluttered.

'Well enough, perhaps,' Anna admitted.

'I've been thinking. That's all.'

'And?'

'I have come to the disagreeable conclusion that after recent events it is not sensible for a person of my age to continue living alone.'

'Oh?' Anna said with astonishment. 'Are you thinking of moving into sheltered accommodation?'

'No, no! Nothing like that. I will stay in my own home, and have someone to live in the house with me.'

'A housekeeper?'

Libby shook her head. 'Not exactly. I do have a cleaner, you know. She looks after most routine things in the house.

No. More of a personal assistant — a PA, I believe they are called? That's what I need. Someone to keep my diary, look after the household budget, pay the bills, negotiate with the insurers, deal with maintenance and repair problems, etcetera. That's what I need.

'Above all, it must be someone I trust, and whose company I find congenial. After all, I must be free to get on with my work. I can't afford unwelcome distractions at my age. I have too much to do.'

Where would such a person be found? Anna wondered. In *The Lady*, perhaps? Through an agency? It would be difficult, very difficult.

'I believe you are such a person, Anna,' Libby said with satisfaction. 'Perhaps such a position would suit you? I would ensure that it paid more than your job with the council, and I believe it might even ease the pain of your recent redundancy.'

For a moment, Anna couldn't believe

what she was hearing. Then it became clear that Libby meant it, every word.

'It would be wonderful, Libby. Thank you. I don't know what to say! But what about my cottage? I have . . . '

'You wouldn't have to live in, although you could do so if you wished. As long as you could be there in the daytime, and at times of great need perhaps, that would be enough. I'm sure we could work something out to suit us both. Anyway, think it over, and please let me know.'

'I will. It's a wonderful proposal, and I would like to accept it. Thank you again! But now there are one or two things I wanted to talk to you about.'

'Let's order a coffee before you start,' Libby suggested, reaching for the little bell on the table.

Anna had been unable to make her mind up in advance about how to proceed. Now she decided to pitch straight in.

'Libby, you told me that you had a baby, a daughter, when you were very

296

young. You also gave me the impression that at a very early stage you lost contact with her, which you now seem to regret. Have I got that right?'

Libby didn't reply. She began to look very tense. Anna hoped what she had to say wouldn't be too great a shock for her, but her course was set now. She had to go on.

'Would it surprise you, Libby, to learn that your daughter lives nearby, and that she has a son, who also lives quite close?'

After a few moments of silent reflection, Libby cleared her throat and said, 'Perhaps I misjudged you, Anna. I did not expect you to go poking around in my personal history.'

'Believe me, Libby, I didn't! It's just that at the time of the flood things happened, and people said things, that started to form a pattern. I couldn't believe it at first, but in the end I had to believe it, and I needed to get a few things straight.

'You see, Libby, I'm engaged now to

marry your grandson. That's the most important thing I wanted to tell you today.'

41

It took a moment. Then Libby smiled and said, 'David Wilson? You have my very best wishes and hopes for the future, my dear. And I must congratulate your fiancé.'

'You knew?'

'About Lydia and David? Yes. I did. Their being in the area was part of the reason for my returning here.'

'Yet you never said anything, to them or to anybody else?'

Libby shook her head. 'How could I? It was far too late for me to go interfering in their lives.'

'So they were why you kept a low profile after you returned to Carlton?'

'Of course.'

Anna took a moment or two to digest all this. She was staggered. The situation was extraordinary. Almost beyond comprehension.

'Libby, David and Lydia know who you are, too. They have kep their distance from you for much the same reason, I believe, but I think they might be interested in meeting you.'

'It's too late,' Libby said.

'No, Libby it isn't! It's not too late a all. The past can't be undone, but al that really counts now is the present and the future. Would you like to mee them?'

Libby gave it some thought before saying, 'Do you know, Anna? I believe would. Perhaps something can be salvaged, after all.'

'I'm sure it can. Family is family, Anna said firmly. 'I will speak to Lydia and David.'

* * *

'Meet Mother? Of course I would like to do that,' Lydia said simply. 'I've longed for that all my life!'

Anna didn't know whether it would

be her or Lydia who burst into tears first.

* * *

David was . . . David.

'Yes,' he said shyly. 'What a good idea. Let's do it!'

* * *

'Make it Friday,' Libby said. 'We'll meet in Sunnyside House on Friday.'

Anna nodded approval. 'As your new PA, I will put that in your diary. What time? Shall we say for morning coffee, or afternoon tea?'

'Morning, I think. That's when I'm at my best.'

'Libby,' Anna said with a chuckle, 'you're never at anything but your best!'

They spoke a little more about the arrangements. Then Anna said, 'There is one more thing we could consider, Libby.'

'What's that?'

'Well, if this is to be a genuine clearing of the ground, perhaps we should think of inviting Lydia's father, too? I'm sure Fred would love to meet his daughter and grandson. He is a lonely old man without any family, or so he believes.'

Anna wondered if she had dared to go too far. There was a stunned silence. Libby's face grew taut, perhaps with anger.

'You knew?' Libby asked.

Anna nodded.

'Does everybody know?'

'No, of course not. But the people who were young with you seem to know, even if they have kept quiet. Liza Tully, Walter McKenzie, and so on. And Fred himself, of course.'

Libby thought it over a little longer. Then she nodded approval. 'You're quite right, Anna. Everything you say is true, and right. We'll ask Fred Baker, too. Let's break the ice.'

'Another note for the PA diary!' Anna

said happily. 'We're doing very well already, Libby.'

'Indeed.' Libby nodded. 'And what you have told me this morning about you and David is wonderful news, Anna. Just perfect! It makes my offer to you even more appropriate. You and David should consider things together now, because one day this old house will be his — and yours.'

* * *

'I wondered if I would ever find out what happened,' Fred said. 'I did wonder. I heard things, of course, but no-one ever said anything to me. She just vanished.'

'You didn't know she carried your child, Fred?' Anna asked.

'Not for sure.' He shook his head. 'No-one said.'

Anna felt like shaking her head. 'And now,' she said instead, 'you have the chance to meet Lydia, your daughter and your grandson all together at last.

Do you want to do that, Fred?'

'Oh, yes!' he said huskily, his eyes gleaming with emotion. 'I do.'

'Friday, then. I'll come for you, and take you up to Sunnyside House.'

'Thank you kindly, Anna. I'd appreciate it if you would.'

★ ★ ★

When Friday came, Anna and David checked that things were in order in Sunnyside House and then got ready to start bringing Libby and the others. Anna closed the front door and joined David, who was standing at the top of the steps looking out across the still flooded garden.

'Ready?' he asked.

She nodded and put her arm in his. They stood still for a moment.

Anna said with a chuckle, 'I'm pleased Libby will get to see her lake before it disappears. She would have been disappointed to miss it.'

'And I'm looking forward to

acquainting myself with my grandparents,' David said.

'And your mum? What will she be thinking?'

He shook his head. 'But I do know she won't be thinking about the time we've all lost. Thanks to you, Anna, she'll be looking forward to the time we still can have together. Come on! Let's make a start.'

She smiled and clutched his arm even tighter, and then they set off.

As they neared their car, Anna said, 'I was thinking, David. Why don't we have a thanksgiving service in the church to celebrate the fact that we lost no-one in the floods? I'm sure lots of people will come to that, church members or not.'

'What a good idea! Is this you speaking as Libby's PA, though, or as the future Mrs Wilson?'

'Does it matter?' she asked with a smile. 'There's only one me.'

'Indeed there is!' David replied. 'And how lucky I am to have found you at last.'

We do hope that you have enjoyed reading this large print book.

Did you know that all of our titles are available for purchase?

We publish a wide range of high quality large print books including:
Romances, Mysteries, Classics
General Fiction
Non Fiction and Westerns

Special interest titles available in large print are:
The Little Oxford Dictionary
Music Book, Song Book
Hymn Book, Service Book

Also available from us courtesy of Oxford University Press:
Young Readers' Dictionary
(large print edition)
Young Readers' Thesaurus
(large print edition)

For further information or a free brochure, please contact us at:
Ulverscroft Large Print Books Ltd.,
The Green, Bradgate Road, Anstey,
Leicester, LE7 7FU, England.
Tel: (00 44) 0116 236 4325
Fax: (00 44) 0116 234 0205